T0374451

INTO THIN AIR

HAILEY ROSE

INTO THIN AIR

iUniverse books may be ordered through booksellers or by contacting:

iUniverse
1663 Liberty Drive
Bloomington, IN 47403
www.iuniverse.com
1-800-Authors (1-800-288-4677)

Because of the dynamic nature of the Internet, any web addresses or links contained in this book may have changed since publication and may no longer be valid. The views expressed in this work are solely those of the author and do not necessarily reflect the views of the publisher, and the publisher hereby disclaims any responsibility for them.

Any people depicted in stock imagery provided by Thinkstock are models, and such images are being used for illustrative purposes only. Certain stock imagery © Thinkstock.

ISBN: 978-1-5320-0288-5 (sc)
ISBN: 978-1-5320-0289-2 (e)

Library of Congress Control Number: 2016912069

Print information available on the last page.

iUniverse rev. date: 07/22/2016

DEDICATED TO...

...the person that is reading this. I just
thought you deserved a dedication for once.
So, here you go. Dedicated to you.

CHAPTER 1

Running Through My Mind

I feel the lukewarm water dripping off of my feet as I jog out of the water with my surfboard resting under my arm.

"Oh! And there you have it, folks. That's the end of today's surfing competition. Come back tomorrow for the sandcastle contest," the speakers echo across the pretty white sand that covers all of Laguna Beach.

"Okay, is it just me or did I totally just flunk that competition?" I say, laughing to my half-sister, Leslie, as we pull off our dark gray wetsuits. My sister and I like to surf, but we aren't just surfers; we are Nepos.

Nepos originate back to the 1800s in my family. Leslie and I have the gift of hydrokinesis; we can control liquid with our minds and make it do whatever we want. Yeah, I know. Sounds awesome, right? Well, it is. But being Nepos does come with some challenges, like the fact that we go to a normal high school, with normal kids, and we have to try to fit in because nobody can know what we are.

"Hey, guys, over here!" our one and only best friend, Julian Garcia, who is also Nepos, calls out from John's Surf Shack. Though he would rather not, he works there after school most days. The Surf Shack isn't necessarily the nicest place around, but, considering that it was built over eighty years ago, it's all right. Oh, who am I kidding? It looks like a dumpster behind one of those trailer pubs that bikers go to all the time.

"Perfect timing!" Leslie screeches excitedly as we run up to Julian, "I was just telling Andrea how amazing I did tonight."

Ever since she was little, Leslie's always been really persistent and boastful, and, I swear, every time she wins something, she never lets me forget it. She brags so much that it gets to the point where either Julian or I have to throw in a sarcastic comment for comic relief, to keep each other from getting a headache.

Don't get me wrong, though. When Leslie's in a good mood, she's really nice and kind to everyone. Even the people Julian and I don't like very much, so that also gets on my nerves. I guess it's good, though. If we didn't have anyone nice in our friend group, we wouldn't be able to function.

"Yes, everyone knows you got thirty points from the judges," Julian says as he hands me my favorite drink, Coconut Berry Juice.

Coconut Berry Juice is honestly, to me, the best drink in the entire universe. It consists of strawberries, bananas, blueberries, and of course, coconut sprinkled on top of everything. The way the thick mix of colors just sits there in the cup, it makes a grin spread across my face.

"Oh, come on. No one's going to congratulate me on getting the score of twenty-four?" I hiss at them while taking a sip of the juice.

"You always get twenty-four," Julian and Leslie answer at the same time.

"I would be better at surfing if you let me cheat, Leslie."

"Awkward," Julian adds, laughing.

I swear, Julian always says that at the most random times; it doesn't even make sense.

Every time we enter a surfing competition, I want to use my powers to my advantage and cheat my way to the finish line by moving the waves towards me, but Leslie insists cheating is a terrible way to honor our powers. I always get the urge to cheat, but I know Leslie would notice. And Leslie's the boss in our family, even though she's a year younger than me.

By the time the three of us start walking back to our apartment, the sun is beginning to set. We share an apartment because all of our parents have been killed by the Praetor, except Leslie's father; he left when she was just a baby. None of us knows why he left, though. Leslie and I have the same mother, but my dad was just a random hook up a year before my mom got married to Leslie's father. The two of us grew up with only our mother.

Our parents died in a war between the Praetor and the Medicus. I don't know much about the war, but I do know that the Nepos species is endangered, because we don't have any more Medicus to protect and heal us. As of today, September, 5th, 2055, there are only a few thousand Nepos left in the United States.

We walk up to the metal apartment door.

"Can you hand me the key?" I ask.

"Yeah, one second," Julian answers, digging through his old, raggedy jean pocket.

I unlock the door and turn on the light before looking around at our apartment. I'm pretty proud of us for having such a decent place. The walls are covered in silver metal, the flooring is light blue metal, and the refrigerator on the left side of the room has, for some odd reason, dark mahogany wood on the outside.

I grin at our apartment and jump onto the squeaky, plaid-patterned pull-out couch. But, before I can even get my pajamas on, I notice the street light shining in from the large window behind the couch, like it always does.

"Do you see that?" I point to the light gleaming in from the window.

"The light? I know. It always keeps me awake," Julian responds.

"No, not the light; the shadow."

"What shadow?" Leslie interrupts.

"At the bottom of the street lamp," I say, worrying.

I'm seeing a shadow of what looks like a man smoking a cigar of some type. It may seem normal to see a shadow in the street, and it is. But the shadow of this man seems familiar. Not in a good way, either.

Julian and Leslie ignore my frightened expression and go to bed. That's just like them. They're both caring people, but they have a tendency to be oblivious to my feelings.

With the confusing thoughts of the shadow running through my mind, I know I'm going to be the only one getting hardly any sleep tonight.

CHAPTER 2

Shotgun

I wake up to someone shaking me continuously. It feels like my brain is trying to make its way out of my head.

"Andy, wake up!" Leslie shouts into my ear.

"Just a couple more minutes," I mumble, throwing a pillow over my head. Mornings are definitely not my thing. Never have been; never will be.

"Andrea Lynn Brookes, get your butt up!"

I open my eyes to see Julian and Leslie standing in front of me, holding their backpacks.

Oh my gosh. I forgot school starts today! As I hop off the couch, I grab two slices of bacon, a glass of Sunny D, and half a piece of burnt toast that's waiting for me on the kitchen counter.

"Darse prisa," Julian says impatiently as he points towards the clock.

"You don't have to speak in Spanish just because you're Mexican," I retort, as I throw a baggy green t-shirt and some stain washed jeans on over my bathing suit and bolt out the door. Julian would never admit it, but he doesn't even know Spanish; he just thinks that he's super cool for knowing ten words.

"I call shotgun!" Leslie yells after giving me a dirty look. Even though I've tried many times, Julian is still the only one with his own car and license. I always get stuck sitting in the backseat because Julian has a not-so-secret 'thing' for Leslie now.

I jump into the back of Julian's rusty, old, tan station wagon and almost drop my bacon while getting in. I glance at Leslie and see her putting in her favorite One Direction CD. This CD is so old; I don't know why she likes it. It came out in 2013, and it's now more than forty years later.

"Not this again," I say to myself, gulping down the rest of my Sunny D. I have to listen to Julian and Leslie sing for ten excruciating minutes before we arrive at school. I honestly don't why they love this music so much.

When I get out of the car, I see him: the man of my dreams. The boy I've liked since he was in my first surfing lesson. Nash Olmstead is standing right there, leaning against the flag pole. Immediately, my heart starts pounding. Just looking at his tall, muscular figure, and his luscious blonde hair gives me the chills.

Okay, try not to freak out, I think, while taking my light brown hair out of the messy bun it's tied up in. I flip my hair around in the wind, only to notice that Julian and Leslie are both staring at me, holding in their laughter.

"Aw, how cute. Andy still has a crush on Nash," Julian jokes.

I punch Julian hard in the side. "Shut up!"

Leslie grins and says, "She wants to marry him and become Mrs. Andy Olmstead."

Julian gives Leslie a loud high five, and they hurry over to Nash to tell him something.

Oh, no. Please, no. While looking down at the ground, I try to walk past Nash as fast as I can without making eye contact, but someone grabs my arm; it's Nash.

"Hey, Andrea, I heard you think I'm cute."

My pale face turns bright red, I croak, "Um, yeah," and then scurry into the school. I honestly don't think I've ever been so embarrassed in my entire life.

As I am walking into class, I can't help but think I might never recover from this experience. The way he looked at me, I couldn't tell what he was thinking. Does he think I'm unattractive and awkward? I hope not.

I couldn't focus in any of my classes because all I could think about was how to get revenge on Julian and Leslie.

I'm in the middle of third period, Chemistry, when something hits me in the back; it's a colossus paper wad. I turn around and see Victoria Wellmington, the Queen Bee at Laguna Beach High School. Her obnoxiously perfect complexion and long, straight hair makes me roll my eyes.

"Excuse me, Andrea, right?" she says with a serious look.

I look at her, puzzled. What could she want from someone like me?

"So, I heard you were flirting with my boyfriend. Don't do it again."

I see her stand up from her seat, and she walks over to me as I look up at her with a scowl. She glares at me before raising her arm and slowly dumping the beaker containing her chemistry experiment all over my head. She plops herself back down at her seat, snickering with her clique of brats.

My mouth falls open as the goo drips off of my face. I restrain myself from whipping the experiment back at Victoria with my mind. Trust me, I really want to douse her in the green goopy experiment consisting of corn starch, H_2O, and green dye, but I can't. My powers would be exposed to the entire classroom if I act on it.

"Victoria!" Mr. Oliver yells, "Office, now!"

Victoria walks out of the classroom laughing in her bogus girly laugh.

"Ms. Brookes, you may go to the bathroom to dry off," Mr. Oliver reports to me.

"Thanks," I answer, storming out of the classroom.

As I walk down the hallway to the bathroom, I look up at the ceiling. I've never really noticed before, but the ceiling has a beautiful mural painted on it. It's a painting of a young woman that looks to be a mermaid, wearing nothing but pink shells. The girl has long, red hair, and she's holding a wand. The painting is amazing, don't get me wrong, but I'm wondering what relevance it has to my school. The only thing I can think of is that whoever painted this mural could know something about magic. I'm probably wrong, though. I tend to overthink things way too much.

Anyway, as I reach the end of the hallway, I shove open the bathroom door and kick all of the stall doors open, to make sure that no one's in the bathroom with me. I stand in front of the mirror and focus all of my attention on the liquid in my hair. I close my eyes, to make the connection stronger, and it starts to gather together. It hovers in midair in front of me in a clumped green ball. Slowly, I move the ball through the air and guide it into the sink. The mixture slides down the sink, making a gross gurgling noise. After it's completely washed down the drain, I head back to third period, completely dry.

I slumbered through the rest of the class. The bell rings, and I snatch my lunch from inside my locker. I walk into the cafeteria to see Julian sitting all alone at our table by the dumpsters. Yes, we do sit by the dumpsters. No, it's not that bad. I kind of like it, actually. This way we can throw away our trash without standing up. Shuffling over, I sit down next to Julian.

"Hey, where's Leslie?" I ask.

"Right here!" Leslie calls out from behind me, holding a giant water bottle.

"What's with the bottle?" Julian chuckles. Before she can answer, I grab the bottle out of her hands and squirt both of them with it. They rub their eyes and give me angry looks.

"Ha! Serves you right!" I say, happier now that I have gotten my revenge.

After school, we all hop into the station wagon and drive over to the beach. I slide out of the car and into the hot sand.

"Look at me; I'm Andy," Leslie snickers, flipping her dark brown hair.

Julian mocks Nash's voice, "Come on, Mrs. Olmstead; let's go over to the Surf Shack."

I roll my eyes. "Seriously, guys, not funny."

Julian slips his 'John's Surf Shack' t-shirt over his head and stands behind the cash register. He hands me a tall glass of Coconut Berry Juice, and I'm done with it in less than a minute. One of the good things about Julian working at the Surf Shack is that I get a dollar off of every drink I order. I'm considered family to Julian, so I get the family discount. I always try to make Julian give me food and drinks for free, but he says that's wrong; he doesn't want me to break the rules. He's always been a hypocrite in that way.

When Leslie's done with her strawberry smoothie, she and I grab our surfboards and head out into the water. The water feels unseasonably cold for the fall, but it feels great.

I paddle as fast as I can, trying to pass Leslie. Ever since we were little, we've always tried to beat each other at everything. I don't know if that's just a sister thing, but Leslie usually wins, and losing is never a good feeling.

Leslie starts paddling faster.

"Ha-ha, I beat you!" she chimes at me.

"Oh, you just wait until the wave comes!" I call back.

We spend the next two hours taunting each other and messing with the water. I peer over at the shore and pretty much everyone had left. I turn back towards the ocean to see a giant, dark wave coming right at me. I see Leslie getting ready to ride the wave and make a fool out of me once again. I focus on the middle of the wave and cause it to shrink. Leslie slips off of her board and I see her crash into the dark water.

"Hey, I know you did that!" she fumes when she resurfaces.

I start to laugh, but before I can take a breath of air, she makes a wave splash me so hard that I go under water. It feels like I'm underwater for ten minutes, but it's really only five seconds. I swim up and my board isn't attached to my ankle anymore.

"Leslie, what'd you do with my board?" I ask angrily.

Before she can answer me, there's a deep rumble from the sky. Leslie and I exchange worried glances and swim back to shore as fast as we possibly can. We both know how dangerous thunderstorms can be. Especially when you're in the water. Last year, Julian was just seconds away from being hit by lighting in the ocean. Thankfully, he ran onto shore just before the lightning struck. Now every time any of us hears thunder or sees lightning while at the beach, we all get a little on edge.

"Come on, guys, my shift just ended, and I think there's a storm coming." Julian motions for us to come over to the car.

On the ride home, when we're all arguing about what happened to my board, out of nowhere, we hear a crash and the car stops suddenly.

"Did you just hit somebody?" Leslie accuses as her eyes widen.

Julian and I hop out of the car, and I can't believe what's in front of me. No, what I'm seeing is not a person; it's worse than that.

"What in the world?" I stare, surprised. It's my surfboard; it has no scratches, and it's in perfect condition.

"What's this?" Julian picks up a blue sticky note that is stuck to the front of my surfboard and reads the note out loud, "*You have a week to get out of California....*"

We look at each other in disbelief.

"This is stupid." I shake my head, trying not to show how freaked out I really am. The fact that my surfboard was recovered from the ocean and then appeared out of thin air is not normal. I'm praying that it's just a prank.

"What is it?" Leslie shouts from the car.

The rest of the ride home Julian and I have to try to convince Leslie that what happened is probably just a joke so she would stop panicking. Believe it or not, Leslie's even more neurotic than I am.

I'm pretending not to be scared out of my mind, but in reality I think I'm going to pee myself. It brings back so many memories seeing this note; I've never seen it before, but my mother used to get notes like this. I used to spy on her at night when I was supposed to be sleeping, and, every once in a while, I'd see her crying over one. I never did figure out what it was or who sent the notes.

When we walk into the apartment building and start to head up the stairs, I hear a noise. I look behind me, but there's nothing there.

"Did you guys hear that?" I look at Julian and Leslie.

"Hear what?" they both wonder.

"It's probably nothing," I tell them, trying to convince myself that was the case.

Julian unlocks the apartment door, and Leslie whips up some pancakes for dinner.

"Your pancakes are so good; I think I'm melting inside," Julian says like he's in love with the food.

Leslie is the chef of the house, but to be honest I don't think her pancakes are all that great. I'm guessing Julian just says that because he has a crush on her.

"Yeah, they're okay for a fifteen-year-old," I snarl.

"What do you mean 'okay'? They're beyond okay," Julian assures, smiling at Leslie like she's a cute puppy or something.

After we're all done eating, I have to do the dishes because, apparently, it's my night to do them. I stick all the dishes in the dishwasher, change into my pajamas, and jump on to the pull-out couch next to Leslie.

Julian comes over and plops down onto his spice brown leather bed (a.k.a. the recliner). The three of us stay awake until about 12 a.m., talking about a bunch of stuff that I can't even remember, until we realize it's only Monday and we have school tomorrow. I completely forgot about school again. It's just now sinking into my mind that summer is actually over; no more late-nights talking about nonsense anymore.

"Night, guys," Julian whispers as he switches off the antique lamp.

CHAPTER 3

Peach Fuzz

I hear someone slide the curtains open as I began to wake up.

"Ow!" I cover my eyes to convey that I'm being blinded by the bright sunlight that's coming in from the steel window.

"Oops. Sorry," Julian responds insincerely as he walks into the bathroom.

"Scrambled, fried, or sunny side up?" Leslie asks as she walks over to me, holding an egg carton.

"Fried," I answer, my mouth starting to water.

I'm always extremely hungry when I wake up. Oh, who am I kidding? I'm starving regardless of the time of day.

"Fried, please!" I hear Julian shout from inside the bathroom.

I sneak over to the bathroom door. "Hey, Julian, what are you doing in there?"

"Nothing," Julian replies in a suspicious voice. I peek through the crack of the door, and Julian's positioned in front of the sink with a razor in his hand.

"Oh my gosh, Julian, are you shaving? You don't even have facial hair!" I hold my stomach as I start dying of laughter. This is hilarious. Julian hardly even has any peach fuzz.

"Wait. Did you say he's shaving?" Leslie cackles from the kitchen. She darts over while getting her phone ready, opens the bathroom door, and takes a picture of Julian before he can block the camera.

"Hey, delete that!" Julian howls at Leslie. I fall to the ground from laughing too hard, marveling at how weird the two of them are.

A few minutes later, we all make our way over to the glass dining table, and I start to eat my fried egg sandwich while Julian tries to erase the picture off of Leslie's phone.

When we're all done with our breakfast, Julian has gotten the picture off of Leslie's phone and into the trash bin app. Leslie pouts about how she's upset he deleted it, and he recovers the photo for her. Julian's such a pushover when it comes to Leslie.

We head downstairs and I slide into the back of the car. Leslie switches on One Direction again, and the music booms as loud as it possibly can.

"Low fuel," Julian reports after a couple of minutes in the car. The station wagon is super old, so we have to refill the gas tank all of the time. There's probably a leak in the tank or something, but it's not enough of an inconvenience that we've felt the need to fix it.

We pull up to Seven Eleven, and, while Julian fills up the gas tank, I step out of the car and head into the silver, modern-looking gas station. The building has a large, red neon sign that reads Seven Eleven right above the doors. I'm positive you could read the sign from twenty miles away.

"Are you serious?" I accidentally whine out loud as I approach the slushy machine.

"Can I help you?" An old woman from behind the cash register with the name tag 'Betty' swaddles over to me. She's wearing jeans with a stretchy waistband, and a long, fuzzy pink sweater with a cartoon cat on it. I hold in my laughter; I love old people.

"Oh. Sorry. All the slushy cups are gone."

"I can get you some more, dear." Betty walks into the back room and returns with a stack of cups.

"Thanks," I say gleefully. I pile up my Mountain Dew slushy to the tippy top and continue to the cash register to pay.

I walk outside after receiving my change and hear someone yell, "Andy!"

I look behind me to see that no one is there. What the heck? At first, I think I recognize the voice, but maybe not. I run up to the car and dive into the backseat.

"Did you call my name?" I ask.

"No," Leslie responds.

"Did you, Julian?"

"Did I what?" Julian petitions.

"Did you call my name? I know someone did."

"I didn't."

We pull away from Seven Eleven and, as I'm looking out of the window, I see something: a man in a black trench coat with a cane. My heart fills with fear. I stare, not able to take my eyes off him. When we were younger, a few weeks before my mom was taken by the Praetor, Leslie and I kept seeing a man that looked just like that almost everywhere we went.

"Leslie, is that him?" I stammer, glancing at Leslie.

"Is that who?" she shouts back at me over the music.

"Never mind." I shift my eyes back over to where the man was a few moments ago, but he isn't there anymore.

As we drive out of the Seven Eleven parking lot, I quickly shake the fear out of my head. I think I might be going crazy, or hallucinating. I don't know, but I seem to be hearing and seeing a lot of strange things lately.

When we stop in our parking spot at school, I push open the car door and jump out onto the silver parking lot. Julian, Leslie and I scurry into the school together. Julian and Leslie seem happy, but me, I just feel different, like something is off.

"See you guys at lunch," Julian says, pulling open his locker.

I walk over to mine and put in the code.

"23, 2, 30," I whisper to myself. "Seriously?"

It won't open; the latch is stuck at the bottom. I stand at my locker for about five minutes trying to open it, when someone walks up behind me.

"Can I help you with that?" I hear someone say.

When I turn, I see Nash smirking at me. I think I'm going to faint. Nash is looking at me with his heavenly baby blue eyes. Suddenly, all of the weird feelings I felt a few minutes ago are gone. I just feel safe when I look into his eyes.

"Uh, yeah. Thanks," I reply, trying not to pass out. Nash pounds on my locker and it opens up immediately.

"You're welcome." Nash smiles and runs his fingers through his blonde hair. When he smiles, his dimples show on his cheeks and I know that if I look at him for too long, I will faint.

"Thanks again," I begin to say, but stop when I see that he's walking over to Victoria. He hugs her from behind and I force myself to look away. I can't see the two of them together without feeling jealous.

Whatever. I don't need you. I try to convince myself that's how I really feel but it doesn't help at all.

I turn around to get my notebook out of my locker, but instead of seeing my notebook, I see a folded up piece of paper. I grab the paper from my locker and unfold it three times, the paper has writing on it: Dear Andy, get out of California or pay the price. . .

Ignoring my original thoughts and being scared once again, I scrunch the paper up into a ball and shove it into my pocket. This has to be a sick joke. I'm not going to leave California just because a piece of paper suggests that I should.

I quickly grab my notebook from the top shelf of my locker and scramble over to my first period: Algebra. Algebra's the one class I have without Victoria, but it's also the only class that I have with Nash. Right when I sit down at my seat, the bell rings. Phew, I made it.

"All right, class, today we are starting a new group project," Mrs. Santos explains.

Oh, great. A group project. This can't be good. I always get partnered up with Holly, the girl who is way too bubbly, and always wants to sit at our lunch table.

Mrs. Santos keeps going on and on about the worksheet, but I'm not really sure what she's saying because I'm too busy staring at Nash sitting in front of me. I can't help but notice the back of his head is just as attractive as the front. I can imagine that his hair would smell like a wonderful mixture of axe and strawberries.

"Did you hear me, Andrea?" Mrs. Santos questions grouchily.

"Huh?" I say, closing my mouth.

"You're partnered up with Nash."

Oh my gosh. This can't be happening. I can't even speak to him without my face turning completely red.

"Get to work!" Mrs. Santos screams at the class. I look over at Nash and he's heading in my direction.

"Hey, so I guess we're partners." He smiles, pulling a chair up next to my desk.

I just sit there blankly; I don't know what to say.

"So let's get started." Nash takes my notebook and rips out a sheet of paper before setting it back on my desk.

"I don't really know what we're doing," I announce like a complete idiot, staring at the notebook he was just touching. By the way, he smells even better than I originally thought.

Nash explains to me what the project is about, but I still have no idea because I'm staring at him again, unable to focus on what he's saying. I can't help it.

"Can you write it down? I have really sloppy handwriting," he says and hands me the paper he just stole from me with a pencil.

I write our names down on the top right corner of the paper: 'Andy Olmstead and Nash Olmstead.' No! I just wrote Andy *Olmstead*. I erase it as quickly as possible and change it to 'Andy Brookes.'

"Did you just write 'Andy Olmstead'?" Nash asks as he smiles.

My face turns beet red, "No."

The bell rings after what feels like ten hours of Mrs. Santos talking nonsense. I grab my new favorite notebook and head over to second period.

The next two periods were full of thinking about how I could have possibly written Andy Olmstead. I swear I was about ready to bang my head on the wall just to get the thought out of my head, when the bell rang for lunch.

I go out to my locker to get my brown bag full of food.

"Hey! Wait up!" Leslie yells running up to me. "I got a note in my locker earlier."

"Really? I did too. What did yours say?" I wonder.

"It was an anonymous love poem. It asked me to meet behind the bleachers after school." She jumps around excitedly. "What did your note say?"

"Oh. I thought your note would be the same as mine, never mind," I mumble disappointedly. Not that I was wanting Leslie to a get threatening note, but I thought maybe she would be experiencing the same emotions as me.

"Who do you think it is?" Leslie prances back and forth. Her pink flip flops make a loud whooshing noise as she moves around.

"I don't know. I guess you'll have to wait until after school," I answer.

Leslie and I sit down at our table across from Julian. She keeps going on and on about her love note.

As an attempt to ignore the boasting about her secret admirer, I start to people watch. I see a nerdy kid eating a bag of Fritos and playing a spaceship game on his phone. Next to him, I see a girl wearing suspenders and brushing her tangled hair. My eyes drift away from the nerds, and I glance towards the popular table, hoping to see Nash. But, instead, standing next to the table, I see the man in the black trench coat talking to Victoria. My pulse starts to rise. This time I know he is here. I can see him in the flesh.

"Leslie, look," I utter, pointing to the man.

"That's him!" Leslie stands up and shouts so loud that everyone in the courtyard looks at us.

A sudden silence makes all of the eyes in the cafeteria stare at Leslie.

Leslie smiles stiffly and sits back down. "Well, that was awkward."

"Who's *him*?" Julian asks.

"The man we told you about, the one we kept seeing before our mom died," I tell Julian.

"Wait, that's him? Why is he with Victoria?"

"I'm not sure, but we need to find out," I answer, trying to play it cool.

Seriously, what is he doing here? It's starting to freak me out a little. Well, more than a little.

We all went our separate ways to fourth period. After fourth and fifth periods are over, Julian and I head outside and hop into the car to wait for Leslie to get back from meeting her mystery lover. I actually get to sit in the passenger seat of the car this time because Leslie's not here yet. I look over at Julian and he has a gloomy look on his face.

"What's wrong?" I inquire.

"Oh, nothing," Julian whines quietly, looking like he's holding back tears. "It's just, I don't want Leslie to find her anonymous lover and end up dating him or something."

"I always knew you were in love with Leslie," I say, reaching over to give him a hug.

"What? I don't like Leslie. What are you talking about?" Julian yells, pushing me away from his large frame.

I've never seen Julian so angry and upset at the same time. It's kind of scary, to be honest. He must really love her, more than he probably knows.

"Julian, it's okay. I won't tell her," I soothe.

"Leave me alone!" Julian jumps out of the car and slams the door behind him.

I get out of the car and close the door silently. I start to follow him; I want to know where he's going. I sneak behind a wall and watch as Julian approaches the bleachers. What is he doing? Is he really going to interrupt Leslie and her secret admirer? I tiptoe close enough to the bleachers so that I can hear every word that they're saying.

"Leslie, come on, let's go home. Your mystery man isn't coming," Julian says.

"What do you mean? Why?" Leslie responds defensively.

"No one will ever love you—"

"Julian!" Leslie wails with anger written all over her tan face. "How could you say that?"

"No one will ever love you . . . as much as I do." Julian tucks Leslie's dark hair behind her ear.

I can't believe this is finally happening. It took him long enough.

I look behind me to make sure no one can see me spying on them, and what I see is a snobby looking girl with her hair in a ponytail glaring at me. She's standing with an adorable little kid; most likely her little brother. Even though she's creeping me out, I ignore the fact that she is there and look back over at Julian and Leslie. What I see is even more strange than the girl herself; Julian and Leslie are kissing.

"Don't tell Andy okay?" Leslie pleads as she bites her lip.

"I won't, at least not yet. Let's go home," Julian says, grabbing Leslie's hand. I run back to the car as fast as I can and hop back into the passenger seat.

A few moments later, Leslie skips up to my window, happier than ever, and demands, "Get out of my seat."

"Fine." I smile, because I know why she's happy.

The entire ride home Julian doesn't say one word to me; I think he's still mad at me. I don't know why he's still mad at me if I was right all along. Maybe it's just a guy thing.

We pull into the apartment parking lot and I hop out when I see a fluffy gray cat sitting by the bushes.

"Aww!" I point the cat out to Leslie.

"Oh my gosh, that cat's ADORABLE!" Leslie screeches.

I walk over to the cat and it starts to run away, but, as soon as I begin petting it, it sticks it's butt up into the air. I bring the cat inside and give it a can of tuna. This is the only time I'm glad that we have tuna in the house. Julian loves it, which is nasty.

"We should name it," Leslie suggests while scratching the cat's back.

"We need to find out if it's a boy or a girl first," I express.

"Ew!" Leslie squeals.

"Don't be a baby." Julian walks over to us and flips the cat over. "Boy," he announces.

"Aww, let's name him Tom," I say, rubbing under Tom's chin. I put him back outside as Leslie walks into the kitchen.

"Any dinner ideas?" Leslie asks, looking over at Julian and me.

"Let's just order pizza," Julian suggests, not even considering if that sounds good to me.

I see Leslie pick up her cell phone up of the table.

"Yes, I would like one medium pepperoni pizza, please," she orders cheerfully after dialing the number.

I'm happy for Julian and Leslie, but, seriously, can they stop being so peppy and annoying? It's really starting to give me a headache.

I slide over to the sink in my fuzzy socks and grab a glass cup. I focus on a water jug and make a big stream of water glop into my cup.

The doorbell rings. "Pizza delivery!" a man yells from the other side of the door twenty minutes later.

I grab some cash out of my pocket and slide over to the door. But, when I open the door, it's not the normal pizza guy. It's the man with his signature trench coat and cane.

"That'll be twenty dollars," he says with a creepy grin.

I gulp. How does he know where I live? And most of all, why is he stalking me? I freeze, hand him the money, grab the pizza box, and slam the door in his face. I turn around to see Leslie standing there with her jaw hanging to the floor.

"Was that who I think it was?" she whispers.

Before I can say anything, Julian comes out of the bathroom wiping his hands on his pants. "Pizza!" he cheers and grabs the box out of my hands.

"I don't think we should eat it," Leslie counters.

"Why not?"

"It was the man who delivered it," I interrupt.

Julian doesn't say anything in response to me.

"Are you seriously giving me the silent treatment?"

"The man in the trench coat?" he guesses, looking at Leslie.

"Yeah," she says worriedly.

I snatch the pizza box back from Julian and set it on the table.

"Open it," he barks.

I open the box and attached to the top is a blue sticky note, just like the one that was on my surfboard.

Leslie rips the note off the box and reads it out loud, "*I know you got the note in your locker, and I know your secret.*" She looks up at me. "The note in your locker was from the man? Why didn't you tell me?"

"I didn't know for sure. Plus, I was going to tell you, but you were so excited about your love note. I didn't want to ruin it for you." I grab the note from her and shove it into my pocket with the other note.

"Forget about the love note; we need to focus on the note you got," she grumbles, "I'm starting to panic; we don't know what this man is capable of."

"Okay, let's not panic; we'll figure it out," I respond, trying to convince myself that I'm not afraid, too.

She jumps onto the couch. I see her give Julian 'the look' and he sits down beside her.

After half an hour of deliberating about what the man wants from us, I scoot back over to the pizza box. I don't really care if this pizza is poisoned; I'm hungry, and maybe it will end my suffering of seeing Leslie and Julian cuddling. I grab a slice of the pizza and bite into it. Surprisingly, it tastes fine.

"What are you doing? It could be poisoned," Leslie warns. I sit down on Julian's recliner and start to eat another slice.

"I don't care; I'm hungry."

"I hope it is poisoned," Julian says under his breath.

"Julian! Don't say that!" Leslie hits him in the shoulder.

After I'm done eating, I go into the bathroom and change into my pajamas. When I come out of the bathroom, Julian isn't on the couch anymore.

"Where's Julian?" I yawn.

"He's outside trying to find the cat, I think," Leslie says, pulling the couch out into a bed.

I walk outside and find Julian sitting on the bench outside the building door.

"Hey, you okay?" I ask as I sit down next to him.

"I'm not talking to you," he grumbles.

"I know, but can't you at least tell me *why*?"

"I can't talk to you because, if I do, I'll end up telling you what Leslie told me not to tell you."

"What did she tell you not to tell me?" I ask calmly, already knowing the answer.

"This is exactly why I didn't wanna talk; I knew you would ask." He continues to avoid eye contact and throws a pebble into the parking lot.

"It's fine, Julian, I know you guys kissed," I admit.

"She told you?" he gawks at me with his brown eyes.

"No, I was sort of . . . spying."

"What? You saw us and didn't say anything?" He starts to raise his voice. I look at Julian and it looks like he's about to cry, again. Ugh. Why is he so emotional lately?

"I wanted you guys to tell me yourselves," I confess, while Julian grabs another pebble and chucks it into the pond next to our apartment building.

"Whatever," he says under his breath. Why can't he just listen to me? He never listens.

After a few minutes of sitting in silence I give Julian a one-sided hug and go back inside. When I walk in, I see Leslie already asleep on the bed, so I hop on it next to her.

Ten minutes later, I hear Julian come in and lie down on his recliner.

"Andy?" I hear him whisper to me.

"Yeah?" I answer.

"Thanks for caring."

CHAPTER 4

Into Thin Air

I had dozed off for an hour and was in the middle of a dream about Coconut Berry Juice, when I woke up to the noise of Julian and Leslie fighting.

"It was a mistake!" Leslie hollers.

What was a mistake? I think to myself, while closing my eyes and pretending to still be asleep.

"Our kiss wasn't a mistake!" Julian shouts in a nasally voice.

"I don't even like you, Julian! I like someone else!" she screams, runs outside, and slams the door behind her.

I hear the sound of Julian sniffling and I slowly stand up. Is he seriously crying again? Wow.

"Seems like I have to keep cheering you up," I joke.

"She said she doesn't like me," he mutters, rubbing his eyes.

"I think she's just confused."

"But you heard her, she said she doesn't like me." He goes into the bathroom and closes the door behind him.

Two hours pass, and Leslie still isn't home.

"We should probably go look for her; it's one in the morning," I state. I'm not too concerned about Leslie. She likes to pull little stunts like this, but sending her to school without any sleep is never a good idea.

"Fine." Julian stands up.

I grab a flashlight and we head out the door, into the darkness. I switch on my flashlight as we walk outside. Once we're outside, I hear something; it sounds like a faint scream. That definitely sounded like Leslie. My stomach starts to churn. It feels like there are a million tiny little people running around in my intestines.

"What was that?" I choke.

"Was that a scream?" Julian breathes. We scamper around the neighborhood for half an hour before we decide to go down to the beach.

"Julian, look." I point to two figures standing by the water. He follows me onto the sand and we inch closer to the figure.

"I think that's her," he whispers.

"It's definitely Leslie, but who's with her?"

My heart starts to race when I realize who it is; the man in the trench coat is standing there, gripping Leslie's arm.

"Julian, it's him."

Before I can react, he starts sprinting towards them and shouts, "Stay away from her!"

I'm stunned. I can't believe he just did that. He's always been the shy one. I run to catch up with Julian and I can see Leslie struggling to get away.

My fingers curl in anger and I can see the man's perfect bone structure as we get closer. He tilts his head downward, and his strong jawline twitches as he sees Julian and me approaching. His long, broad nose sits crooked on his face, almost looking like a witch's nose.

"No, you stay away from her!" he hollers at us. He turns and sprints away towards the east side of the road, taking Leslie along with him. She's hanging over his right shoulder like a rag doll. I whimper while looking at Leslie's face. Even from far away, I can feel her pain. She looks so scared, yet there's nothing I can do to help.

Julian and I try to chase after him, but our speed is nowhere near as fast as his, and, a few seconds later, Leslie and the man are out of sight. This can't be happening.

"No!" Julian screams so loud, I think the whole town might have woken up. I look along the shoreline and the road, running my eyes up and down as far as I can see. But nothing. There's nothing.

Julian looks at me with tears streaming down his face, "What are we gonna do?"

Both of us know for a fact that we can't get the police involved. They'd find out that we're living in an apartment together without a parental guardian. If they find that out, we'll all be put in foster care.

Okay, I actually understand why he's crying this time. Seeing him cry makes me want to cry, too. I feel tears start to form, but, deep down, I know I have to comfort him again. I always have to be the strong one.

"I don't know, but we'll think of something," I say as we head back towards the apartment.

We're sitting in the living room in silence, trying to come up with a plan, when I hear something scratch at the door.

"What was that?" Julian murmurs.

"I don't know." I tiptoe over to the door. I look through the peephole, but I see absolutely nothing. I prepare for the worst, and crack the door open to peak my head out.

Tom looks up at me and meows.

"Oh my gosh, Tom, you scared me." I pick Tom up and bring him inside, over to Julian.

Honestly, the only thing that can make me feel the slightest bit better right now is cuddling. I don't want to cuddle with Julian, obviously, so, Tom will have to do for now. I soon fall asleep with Tom's fur tucked around me, keeping me warm and cozy.

I wake up a couple hours later to see him staring at me from the edge of the couch.

"Come on, Andy, we need to get to school," Julian voices from the kitchen. I try to get off the couch, but I fall onto the floor, almost landing on Tom. He darts away from me and into the bathroom.

"We can't go to school. We need to find Leslie," I shoot back.

"Even if we did find her, how would we get her away from the man?" Julian throws his backpack over his shoulder. Wow, for being so in love with Leslie, he doesn't seem to care all that much.

"We can't just give up," I say, zipping up my sweater.

I glide into the bathroom and find Tom sitting next to the bathtub.

"Come on, Tom."

I sweep him up into my arms and make my way outside. I set Tom outside of the apartment building doors, and place myself into the passenger seat of the car. I know I said I wanted to sit in the passenger seat earlier, but it feels weird sitting here without Leslie. My thoughts are shaken from my mind when Julian gets into the driver's side and starts the car.

The car ride to school is really awkward, neither of us says a word. We skid into our parking spot and I open the passenger door before Julian and I walk into the school. We go our separate ways to our lockers, and I put in the code; this time it works on the first attempt. I grab my Algebra notebook and drag myself over to first period.

When I sit down at my desk, Mrs. Santos shuffles over to me. "You're late, Ms. Brookes."

"Well, I'm sorry. It's not my fault my sister disappeared last night," I scoff.

"Get to work," she sneers.

I look to the side and see Nash walking towards me. I really don't want to deal with him right now.

"Did you say your sister disappeared? Is she okay?" Nash asks, pulling out a pencil. I open my notebook and rip a piece of paper out of it.

"I don't know," I grumble. This is the first time I'm not scared to talk to Nash. Maybe it's because I'm too preoccupied thinking about Leslie.

"Oh. Well, I hope she's okay," Nash consoles, grabbing the piece of paper that I ripped out of my notebook. Nash and I didn't really talk for the rest of the period, he just wrote stuff down and stared at me. It was a little strange.

The bell rings and I pick up my notebook.

I start to walk out of the classroom, when Nash calls out, "Hey, Andy, wait up."

I turn around and Nash is running up to me.

"Are you doing anything after school today?"

"I'm gonna go look for Leslie; so, yes, I'm doing something."

I start to walk away from Nash when he says, "Can I come with you?"

I turn around, confused. "Why do you wanna help look for Leslie?"

"I broke up with Victoria earlier; I need to do something to get my mind off of her."

"You can't come, sorry," I exhale in annoyance.

"Oh, why not?" Nash looks at me in the eyes. Why did he have to look at me in the eyes? Now I feel terrible.

"Okay, fine, you can come, but it could be dangerous."

"Dangerous how?" Nash urges.

"I'll explain later. Meet me by the flagpole after school."

I walk over to my locker to put my algebra notebook away, and Nash shouts out from behind me, "Yeah, sure, the flagpole."

I start to freak out a bit; Nash is coming with Julian and me. He doesn't even know Leslie; why would he want to come with us? And I can tell it's not just to 'get his mind off Victoria'.

I start to walk towards second period when I pass Victoria; she gives me the dirtiest look anyone could ever give someone. I give her a smile and try to pass her in confidence, but, instead, I trip on something: Victoria's foot.

"I heard you're trying to steal my boyfriend from me again," Victoria accuses.

I pick myself up, whisper into her ear, "He's not your boyfriend anymore," and strut away.

I felt so cool for a moment. I finally stood up to Victoria. But I couldn't stop thinking about the fact that Leslie was missing.

After second and third period, I walk into the courtyard and see Julian waiting at our table by the dumpster.

"Is it okay if Nash comes with us to look for Leslie after school?"

"Did you really invite Nash to look for Leslie with us?" Julian asks, biting into an apple, "Awkward."

"Really, Julian? Again with the awkward? I didn't invite him; he asked me," I argue.

"Whatever, I don't care if he comes." Julian swallows a piece of his apple.

I know this is a horrible thing to think, but, at this moment, I'm kind of glad Leslie left. Otherwise Nash wouldn't be coming with me to hang out after school.

When lunch is over, I see Victoria walking towards the bathroom, but she gets stopped by one of her friends. Perfect opportunity to spy on her. I need to get some dirt or gossip on her so I can get back at her for dumping the experiment on me. I sprint into the bathroom without Victoria seeing me, and sulk into the third stall. While I'm sitting in the blue metal stall, I hear someone come into the bathroom. It sounds like Victoria's voice, and she's on the phone.

"Dad, you have her, right? Okay, good. I'm dying of thirst. Keep following the other two around until you have an opportunity to snatch them too," Victoria hangs up the phone and walks out of the bathroom after fixing her hair in the mirror.

Wait. What does she mean by do you have *her*? Could she be talking about Leslie? She was talking to her dad, and she said to get the "other two" when he can. Could Julian and I be the other two? If Leslie was taken by the man in the trench coat, that would make him Victoria's dad. She said she was parched.

Oh my god. That must mean that Victoria and the man are . . . Praetor.

I'm so surprised by my own discovery, that I find my mouth is hanging open and I can't move. But I don't have time to process all of this independently; I need to tell Julian immediately. I came into the bathroom to do some harmless spying on Victoria, and I found out some crucial information. My little spy experience ended more successfully than I had planned.

I burst out of the bathroom. I have to find Julian. I look over to see him standing by his locker.

"Julian!" I call out, sprinting up to him. I pull him aside and shove him into the janitor's closet, so no one can hear us. Also, I've always thought it would be cool to have a secret conversation in a janitor's closet.

"Jeez, chill out. What's wrong?" Julian says, laughing as I trip over a mop.

"It's not funny. I heard Victoria in the bathroom and she was talking to her dad on the phone." I'm talking so fast that I'm surprised Julian can even understand me.

"So?"

"Her dad is the man in the trench coat, Julian," I whisper, trying to catch my breath.

"Wait. Are you serious?"

35

"Yes, and she said she was *thirsty*. I think Victoria and her dad are Praetor."

A Praetor is our natural enemy disguised as a human. If they weren't disguised, they'd be very pale; almost translucent. They feed on Nepos blood, and, if they drain one of us completely of blood, we turn into a Praetor, a fate worse than death. If they drink our blood in small amounts, the blood can last for a lifetime. Either way, the man in the trench coat has Leslie right now, and I don't want either of those things to happen to her.

CHAPTER 5

Wellmington

The bell for the end of the school day rings. I sweep over to my locker and grab my backpack. I pass Julian at his locker and we walk out of the school together, looking for Nash.

"There he is." Julian points over to the flagpole.

"You ready to go?" I ask him as we approach.

He nods and follows me over to the car, stopping before getting in.

"Uh, maybe we could just ride in my car," he suggests, looking at Julian's station wagon like it is a ticking time bomb. I smile because I expected that he'd disapprove of the station wagon.

Julian and I follow him across the parking lot and hop into Nash's shiny black convertible.

"I hate rich people," Julian sighs.

Nash laughs, putting on his sunglasses. "Where to?"

"Where does Victoria live?" I ask.

"Why?"

"That's where we're going."

"I'm only doing this to get my mind off of Victoria."

"Just drive," I demand.

Nash speeds out of the parking lot and into the busy street. I look over at Julian and his hair's blowing around everywhere because of the wind. I hadn't realized how long his jet black hair was getting before now. I will have to force him to get a haircut after we find Leslie.

Nash parks on the street in front of Victoria's house a few minutes later and there are no cars in the driveway.

"There's no one home," Nash points out.

"It's better this way." I jump out of the convertible and strut up to the huge, wooden front doors. The doors creak open by themselves. I always see doors open by themselves in movies, but I never thought it would be this creepy in person.

"Come on." I motion to Julian and Nash to follow me.

"Why would Leslie be at Victoria's house?" Nash wonders aloud.

"Just trust me." We all tiptoe onto the cold marble floor. "Is there a basement?"

"Yeah. The stairs are right over there," Nash confirms. I yank open the basement door and step onto the first step.

"Stay up here and make sure no one comes in the house," I order. I sneak down the stairs, and at the bottom of the stairs is another door. I peek through the crack of the door, but there's nothing there, so I open the door and step into the room. It smells of mildew, and it's freezing cold. I can hardly see anything but I manage to croak out, "Leslie?"

No answer. I turn the corner and there's a giant gray box sitting on the floor, in the middle of the large gloomy room.

I lift the lid off, and it's filled with a bunch of blue sticky notes. One of the sticky notes has writing on it, I pick up the note, and it has a list of names on it:

<u>Nepos</u>
Andrea Brookes
Leslie Brookes
Julian Garcia
Holly Attman

Holly Attman, the overly bubbly girl from Algebra class, is Nepos?

I hear something crash from above me. I dash up the stairs, and Julian's standing at the side of the room, trying to sweep up a broken vase.

"Julian, now they're gonna know we've been here," I lecture.

"Well, excuse me," he answers with a little too much attitude.

"I wanna know why we're here," Nash interrupts.

"Should we tell him?" I whisper to Julian after joining him on the other side of the room. If we tell him, he won't believe us and think we're crazy, but, if we don't tell him, he'll just keep asking questions until we do and threaten to tell Victoria we were here.

"He was dating Victoria yesterday. I would guess he already knows. But, if he doesn't, I think it's a bad idea, Andy."

"I'm right here," Nash informs us as he takes the broom out of Julian's hands and puts it away. Unable to come to a consensus with Julian privately, I avoid the decision and head over to the huge vintage-looking spiral stairs.

"I'll come with you," Nash says as he runs up behind me.

I glance back at the bottom of the stairs and Julian's standing there, looking at me with a disapproving expression.

"We have to be fast; Victoria usually gets home at three thirty."

"What time is it now?" I reply.

"Three."

The two of us step on to the top story of Victoria's house. We walk over to Victoria's bedroom and I turn the door handle. When I push the door open, her room alone is the size of our whole apartment. I look around in awe; Victoria's room looks like the master bedroom of a palace. The walls are a light pink metal, and her obnoxiously large bed is pink as well.

"What's in there?" I point to a white arch on the other side of her room.

"Her closet."

I start to walk towards the closet, but pause mid-step when we hear footsteps running up the stairs. We jump behind Victoria's bed. I look over at Nash and realize that I'm super close to him. We're squished together. I never in a million years thought I'd be this close to Nash.

Someone approaches the bedroom door. I swear, if Victoria comes into her room, I'll punch her for dumping that experiment on my head. Well, actually, I wouldn't. But I would really want to.

"Come on, guys! Victoria just pulled into the driveway!" Julian shouts from the other side of the door.

Nash jumps up. "My car's out there."

"Go distract Victoria. Julian and I will sneak out the back," I demand.

We open the door to see Julian impatiently waiting. Julian and I sprint down the spiral stairs and unlock the back slider doors, while Nash stays at the top of the stairs to wait for Victoria.

"Oh, crap. We have to walk back to school to get the car," I say after we make it out of the yard.

"Yeah, I know," Julian answers, annoyed.

We are halfway to the school when he says, "There was no point in going to Victoria's house."

"Actually, there was," I insist, pulling the blue sticky note out of my pocket. I hand it to Julian and he stares at it for a while.

"Holly Attman?" he questions.

"Yeah. I guess she's a Nepos too."

We stumble into our school's parking lot a while later and slide into the station wagon. On the ride home, Julian interrupts my wallowing by saying that we need to get gas. We drive up next to Nash's convertible at Seven Eleven.

"Hey, Nash is here," Julian observes.

I step out of the car and head into the gas station to get a slushy, like I always do while Julian fills up the gas tank. When I open the door, I see Nash standing over by the soda machine.

"So, are you back with Victoria?" I ask casually, hoping the answer is no.

"Definitely not," Nash answers.

"Oh. Why?"

"I have my eye on someone else." Nash grins, filling up his Styrofoam cup with Cherry Pepsi.

Is he talking about me? No, he couldn't be. I grab a 32oz Styrofoam cup and pour Mountain Dew slushy into it.

"What did you tell Victoria you were there for?" I wonder as we head towards the cash register.

"I told her I left my swim shorts there." He pauses. "Why were we really there?"

I say nothing, and hand the cashier, Betty, my money.

I ignore Nash's question, say, "See you at school tomorrow," and bolt out of Seven Eleven as fast as I can. Phew. I dodged a bullet.

When I bounce into the car, Julian asks what Nash said to me, and I have to explain everything to him on the way home. I leave out what Nash had said about "having his eye on someone else", because I don't want to give him false hope for me.

I get out of the car and see Tom sitting next to the bench outside of the apartment building, right where I left him. I swoop him up into my arms and bring him upstairs into the apartment. I set him down on the floor and open a can of tuna. He devours the tuna in about five seconds, and when he's done, it's time for me to eat dinner. It's really frustrating without Leslie here; I don't know what to eat.

"Chips 'n' cheese okay?"

"I guess," Julian mutters. I grab a plate and dump some tortilla chips on it, but when I pull the shredded cheese out of the fridge, it's all moldy.

"Ew, gross!" I yell, throwing the bag of cheese into the trash. "I guess we're just having tortilla chips for dinner."

After we're done with the chips, Julian gets a phone call, and then says, "I have to cover a late shift at the Surf Shack. I gotta leave right now."

He picks up Tom and trudges out of the door. I look around the apartment. I'm all alone. I've never really been here by myself before; Leslie is always here to keep me company while Julian is at work.

I pull my laptop out of the case and search on Google, 'Victoria Wellmington.' All that pops up is a website that has all of Victoria's cheerleading information.

Hmm, maybe I'll just try 'Wellmington.' A site shoots up called *Wellmington's Warehouse Company*. Weird. Why do the Wellmington's own a bunch of warehouses?

I shut off my laptop a while later and decide to try to call Leslie. I don't know why I didn't think of calling her earlier.

After twenty seconds of the phone ringing, I hear Leslie's voicemail: "Hey, it's Leslie. Leave a message and I'll get back to you as soon as I can." Her voicemail always makes me happy because I can hear Julian and I giggling about something that probably wasn't even funny in the background.

But, instead of laughing at it this time, my throat closes up. I miss hearing Leslie's voice. I force the thought that I may never see her again out of my head and distract myself by filling the bathroom sink with water. I focus on the water and make a heart float into the air that has two letters inside of it. The letters are A and N, for Andy and Nash. Yeah, I know; it's cheesy.

I drop the water back into the sink and start to run a hot bath. I slide into the steaming tub and just sit there for a while. Hot baths calm my nerves for some reason.

I start thinking about how, just ten short years ago, Leslie and I were playing in our huge backyard with our mom. We would all play on the swing set at this time every night. It makes me happy, thinking about that.

I pull a towel off of the rack next to the bathtub and wrap myself in it. After I change into my pajamas, I flip off the lights and sit down on the couch. I dial Leslie's number, just to hear her voice again. Right after I call Leslie, the door opens.

"I'm back," Julian whispers.

The loud shower from the apartment next door to us starts running, so I pull a fuzzy blanket over my head and fall asleep after just a few minutes.

CHAPTER 6

Restricted Number

The first thing I see when I wake up is Julian dropping a carton of eggs. I jump off of the couch and run over to clean up the splattered eggs.

"Seriously, Julian?" All of the eggs are cracked. "That was a huge waste of money."

"Hey, I'm the one who makes the money, so don't be complaining," he growls. Julian does make the money, but he doesn't make all of the money. Leslie and I's mom left us money in her will.

I pick up the egg carton and throw it down the trash shoot.

"I'm guessing that was gonna be our breakfast," I say.

He nods.

"Well, that's just miraculous."

I pop a piece of toast into the toaster, and grab a plastic cup with a cartoon turtle on the side of it. I focus my energy on the sink faucet and make water pour out of it into the cup, just because I can.

Julian grabs my cup and gulps all of the water down. "Thanks."

Rolling my eyes, I refill my turtle cup with Sunny D, because Julian hates Sunny D.

When my toast pops out of the toaster, it scares the crap out of me. I jump back and knock Julian onto his butt, which seems impossible to do because I'm 5'7" and he's a little over six feet tall.

"Hey!" Julian yelps.

"Sorry," I apologize, sliding the toast out of the toaster. Grabbing a container of peanut butter from the cupboard, I spread it all over my toast. It may sound gross, but it's actually really good. Once I'm done with the toast in four big bites, Julian stares at me like I'm crazy because I ate it so fast.

I walk over to the dresser and pull out a blue dress with flowers all over it. I feel like dressing nice today. I skip into the bathroom and pull out Leslie's makeup bag. I put a black line of eyeliner on my top eyelid, and some cherry lip-gloss on my lips. I follow Julian out into the parking lot and get into the car.

"Whoa," Julian remarks looking at me with a confused expression.

"What?"

"Why do you look like a girl?" He turns the key to start the engine.

What does he mean 'why do I look like a girl'? I always look like a girl. At least, I hope I do.

"Excuse me?" I answer hitting Julian with my racecar backpack.

"You're wearing makeup. You never wear makeup."

The whole ride to school I glare at Julian, but, sadly, he never sees my award-winning look.

I slump out of the car and Julian and I walk into the school together. Usually, there aren't many people in the hallways because we always arrive at school late, but today we got to school at the right time. It's really strange. There are ton of students at their lockers, and I have to make my way around all of them to get to mine.

I put in my locker combination and it opens on the second try. Once I've swapped my backpack for my Algebra notebook, I head into Algebra class. I walk over to Nash's desk and sit by him, instead of waiting for him to sit by me like he usually does.

"Hey," I speak with confidence. This whole talking-to-Nash thing is getting a lot easier. I guess it's true; wearing a little bit of makeup does make you more confident.

Nash looks up at me. "You look . . . different."

"Different how?" I pretend not to know why I look different.

"You look really pretty."

"Was I not pretty before?" I hiss.

"No, you've always been pretty." He grins awkwardly, choking on his words.

Nash sounds nervous. Did I make him nervous? How is this happening? Did I just make Nash Olmstead, captain of the surf team, choke on his words?

"Oh, well, thanks," I mutter. I pull a pencil from the side of my notebook and start to take notes from the whiteboard.

"I hate this class," he complains a few minutes later.

"I like this class, because you're in it."

Did I seriously just say that out loud? Oh my gosh. Someone shoot me now.

Nash chuckles.

Of course, right when I thought I was getting comfortable talking to him, I had to say that.

My face turns beet red, again, and I think I'm going to faint in front of the entire class. I pretend to scribble down more notes from the board, trying to avoid making eye contact with Nash for the rest of the period.

A few hours later, a bell rings and it is already time for lunch. I forgot to pack a lunch today, so I have to pay a dollar to get school food.

When I get up to the front of the line where the food is served, an old hag puts a pile of slop onto my tray. Well, that's just great. The one day I forget to pack a lunch they're serving piles of crap.

"Hey," I say, sitting down next to Julian.

"Ew, you're eating that?" he questions as he stares at my food, looking like he's going to throw up.

"I forgot to pack a lunch." I look across the courtyard and see Victoria talking to Nash, playing with her hair.

Julian sees me staring at them and says, "You need to get over him. Everyone knows they always get back together."

"They won't get back together if I tell Nash who Victoria really is."

"You wouldn't."

"Wouldn't what?" I hear someone say from behind me. It's Holly Attman, ready to annoy us for the next half hour.

"Oh, hey, Holly." Julian looks at me with a worried expression on his face.

"Should I tell her about the note I found?" I whisper to Julian.

"If you want to."

I pull Holly away from the courtyard and inside the school. I'm about to say something, when I see the man, Victoria's father, standing at the end of the hallway.

"Not him again!" Holly squeaks.

"You've been seeing him too?"

"What do you mean 'too'?" Holly asks.

I then had to explain to Holly that I knew she was Nepos and everything that's been happening this past week. Holly agreed to help Julian and I search for Leslie tomorrow after school, because it's a Thursday and we don't have school this Friday.

I peer into the courtyard and see Julian pointing to the clock, and then the bell rings to go to fourth period. Holly skips away from me as if nothing happened.

I open my locker and grab my Spanish binder. When I turn around, Victoria's standing there.

"Aw, how cute. You're wearing makeup," Victoria says sarcastically.

"What do you want?"

"I just wanted to let you know Nash and I are getting back together, so you can give up on him now." Victoria pushes my binder out of my hands and walks away.

I turn to pick up my binder, when someone picks it up for me. It was the man. I look up at his cold, dark, black eyes and frown. I want to punch, kick, and hit him as hard as I can. I really want to, but I restrain myself.

"Sorry, my daughter can be a bit feisty." He smiles creepily, holding my binder.

I swipe my binder from his arms and shout, "Where's my sister?!"

Everyone in the hallway stops to stare at me, but I don't care; I need the truth. I glare at the man and he just smiles back at me.

"Your sister? I know nothing about that. Sorry, sweetie."

Did he just call me 'sweetie'? That's disgusting.

"Don't play dumb with me; I saw you take her."

Right when he is going to say something in response, the principal comes up behind me. "Office, now, Ms. Brookes."

I glare at the man before walking into the principal's office and sitting down in the squishy red chair in front of his desk.

"What were you doing yelling at Vincent Wellmington?" Mr. Slater, the principal, shouts at me.

Vincent Wellmington. Now I know his name. Thanks, Mr. Slater.

"Oh, nothing," I reply, picking chunks of my black nail polish off.

"You're suspended for the rest of the school day," Mr. Slater demands. I walk out of the office, pretending not to care, but I really do care. What am I supposed to do for the next two hours?

I strut out of the school, not regretting anything. Vincent deserves to be yelled at. He deserves way worse than just being yelled at. If he doesn't return Leslie soon, he's going to be hearing from me. And maybe Julian too.

After I grab my headphones from the station wagon, I decide to take a walk, considering I'm not allowed on school grounds. It's a very rare occasion, me taking a walk. Especially taking one by myself. As I'm walking, I pass by the cute little playground I used to play on when I was younger. Oh, the memories.

When a few minutes pass, I find myself sitting on the beach in front of the waves. I watch the waves shrink and hit the shore. It's a beautiful sight. It really is.

I'm listening to a nice song on my phone. Leslie downloaded this song for me last week. At the time, I told her how dumb the song was. I insisted it was just another lame jazz song. But now, now I'll always remember how I feel in this very moment. The moment that I am without my sister; my other half. The moment that I am so sad, yet so at peace at the same time. The sound of the seagulls put me at ease. There are hardly any people on the beach because most of the people who hang out here are teenagers, and all of the teenagers are in school right now. Excluding my rebel self, of course.

Almost two hours pass, so I start to make my way back to school. Julian will probably be wondering where I am. I walk past the playground again, and, this time, I see a bunch of little children running around and laughing. They're so cute, I just wish I was as happy as them right now. I know I will be soon. As soon as I find my baby sister again.

I walk into the school parking lot and head towards the station wagon. I still have a few minutes until school is out for the day. I just hope Mr. Slater doesn't see me out here in that short interval of time.

I hop on top of the car, still listening to music and see Julian coming out of the school.

"How did you get out here so fast?" Julian asks, getting into the car. I hop off the roof of the car and slide into the passenger seat.

"I got suspended for the last two periods of the day."

"What do you mean?"

"I sort of freaked out on Victoria's dad."

On the way home Julian and I argued over whether or not I should've yelled at him. Julian says I shouldn't have freaked out on Vincent, but, in all honesty, I know he would've done the same thing.

As soon as I unlock the apartment door, my phone rings.

"It says, 'Restricted Number'." I flip on the light and look over at Julian.

"Answer it," he pleads. I press the Answer Call button, and what I hear makes my heart jump out of my chest.

"Andrea?" Leslie's voice cracks from the other side of the phone.

"Leslie, is that you?" I question in disbelief. Julian looks at me with his jaw wide open.

"I'm in LA, in a warehouse or something," she whispers quietly.

"What are you calling me from?" Just then, the phone line fizzes and the call disconnects.

"What happened? Was that Leslie? Did she hang up?"

"She said she's in Los Angeles."

"Los Angeles, that's only an hour away," Julian sputters.

"I know. Let's go," I demand, opening the door.

"We can't go now; we need rest before we hit the road."

"Julian, we have to go now. She's with a Praetor; who knows what could happen."

"Don't you remember? If we miss a day of classes without an excuse, a parent's signature is required. We can go after school tomorrow, and we'll have all weekend to look for her."

"Fine. I'll ask Nash if he knows anything that can help us. We need to get Victoria alone so we can talk to her."

I slump onto the couch. Why do we have to wait until after school tomorrow to look for Leslie? I know it will give us more time to search, but she could be long gone by that time. I guess the only good part is that now we'll have a chance to get Victoria alone and make her tell us where her dad is keeping Leslie.

I get up off of the couch and head into the bathroom to change into my pajamas. When I return to the living room, I see Julian eating tortilla chips for dinner. Again. After grabbing a couple of chips, they're all shoved into my mouth.

"Mmm, that dinner was filling," I state sarcastically. I plop onto the couch and fall asleep to the sound of Julian crunching on chips.

CHAPTER 7

Trespassing

"**H**ere. Have some breakfast." Julian is standing above me with a bag of tortilla chips.

"No, thanks." I shove the chips away, getting up off of the couch. I sulk over to the kitchen and grab a bowl. I dump some Cinnamon Toast Crunch into the bowl and pull a gallon of milk out from the fridge. I unscrew the milk's lid and focus on the milk to make it pour into the bowl with Cinnamon Toast Crunch in it.

"Now this is more like it," I say with a mouthful of cereal.

I throw the cereal bowl in the kitchen sink and walk into the bathroom to put on some cherry lip-gloss after I'm done eating. I come out of the bathroom to get some clothes from out of my dresser, and Julian's looking at me with an odd face.

"Is lip-gloss your new thing or something?"

"Oh, shut up. At least I'm not trying to shave my invisible facial hair," I snap, putting on some ripped jeans and a Mickey Mouse t-shirt.

We walk out into the parking lot and pass Tom sitting by the pond on the way out.

"Morning, Tom," I say, jumping into the car. I knew Julian was worried and lost in thought thinking about Leslie, because, on the ride to school, I blared Nirvana as loud as it could go and he didn't even change it.

I open the car door and fall out onto the school sidewalk, tripping over the curb. Julian walks by me, smirking, and doesn't bother to help me up. I have to run to catch up to him; he left me on the sidewalk to get plowed over by seniors.

The seniors hate us sophomores at Laguna Beach High School because the freshman have their own building. Sophomores are basically like the freshman here. Julian and I walk into the school and head over to our lockers. I'm opening my locker as Holly comes over to me.

"Am I still coming to help look for Leslie after school?" she shrieks excitedly.

"We're going to Los Angeles. You can come if you want," I say, shutting my locker.

"Yes! I'm up for a little road trip," Holly squeals before skipping away. I walk over to first period and set my Algebra notebook down on my desk.

"Am I coming on the road trip to Los Angeles?" Nash pulls a chair up next to my desk and sits down.

"How do you know about it?"

"Holly told me," he states. I don't know if Nash should come, after all, he's back together with Victoria.

"It would be kind of weird with you there, now that you're back with Victoria," I say, grabbing my note paper from yesterday.

"No, I'm not. Did she tell you that?" he questions.

"Oh. Yeah. Then you can come. I guess."

I make it seem like it's not a big deal, even though I'm really excited that he's not back with Victoria.

"Also, I need a favor," I whisper to Nash so the other students won't hear.

"Anything." He grins.

"Get Victoria alone. I need to talk to her—I mean—interrogate her."

He laughs, but in a serious way. "For sure."

Once first period was over, second and third period flew by like a jet. I head over to my locker to get my lunch. After I have my lunch in my hands I walk into the courtyard and see Julian waiting for me at our table. But it isn't only Julian; Nash is sitting next to him.

I sit down at the table and wonder aloud, "What are you doing sitting here, Nash?"

"Julian and I were just discussing whose car we should take on the road trip," he explains, getting up from the table and walking off.

I look over at Julian and he's scolding me with his expression.

"I didn't know he was coming with us until first period," I defend.

"He said Holly's coming too?"

"Yeah, she is. Whose car are we taking?"

"Mine. It has more room," he snarls. Dang it. I want to take Nash's convertible, it's way nicer, and it has air conditioned seats. If you ask me, air conditioned seats are the best thing to own if you live in California.

When Julian and I are done arguing, and lunch is over, we scurry over to our fourth periods. I have Holly in fourth period, and she was talking to me the entire time about how excited she is for the road trip.

In fifth period, there's this peculiar kid, named Malcolm, who just stares at me or reads the entire time. In sixth period, I fell asleep, so I'm not sure what I was supposed to be doing.

I wake up to the sound of bell ringing for the end of the school day. I hurry outside and grab Julian on the way out. I see Nash and Holly standing over by water fountain and I run up to them.

"Ready to go?" I ask. Nash and Holly follow Julian and I over to the station wagon and they both hop into the back of the car.

Holly's phone rings and we have to sit in the parking lot until she's done talking.

A few minutes later she says, "I can't go on the road trip anymore. I forgot I have to babysit my little brother," and jumps out of the car without a goodbye.

"Oh, speaking of forgetting things: I have Victoria locked in the janitor's closet," Nash informs.

"Seriously?" Julian asks, following Nash and me back into the school.

The three of us walk into the closet cluttered with cleaning supplies, and I see Victoria tied to a wooden chair with duct tape covering her mouth.

Julian's mouth drops open in shock, and I just smile, high-fiving Nash for his brilliant work. Honestly though, I can't believe he just tied her up like that. Especially considering he was dating her not that long ago.

"Can you guys leave me alone for a minute?" I ask Julian and Nash.

They head out of the closet hesitantly.

"Now, tell me where your dad took Leslie," I growl, staring directly at Victoria.

Victoria scoots around, trying to tip her chair over, and trying to mumble something.

I rip the tape off of her mouth, not caring about the pain it will cause her. I just want to know where Leslie is.

"I'm not saying anything," Victoria hisses, frowning at me.

"Tell me." I kick the chair, nearly tipping her over.

She laughs, sounding almost exactly like a witch. "My dad just wants to spend time with his other daughter."

My mind scrambles around. Did she just say Vincent is Leslie's dad? I stand there, completely silent. I stare at Victoria for a little while, taking everything in. She doesn't even look remotely scared being tied up to that chair. Her brown, scheming eyes glare back at me.

Finally, I work up the courage to say, "Don't play tricks with me."

"I'm not. He wants her back in the family. Now untie me."

I ignore Victoria's wishes and put the duct tape back over her mouth. She won't be any help. There's no way Vincent is actually Leslie's dad. I won't believe it. I walk out of the closet and shut the door behind me. I see Julian and Nash waiting.

"I'm leaving her in there," I tell them.

I explain to them what Victoria told me minutes ago, and they actually believe it. There's no way Leslie is related to that monster. No way.

CHAPTER 8

It's Just a Dream

Julian and Nash look at each other with worried expressions on their faces as Julian starts the car and I continue telling them all the reasons why Victoria deserves to die in that closet. They probably think I'm going insane, but I'm not. I just want my sister back.

About halfway to Los Angeles we have to stop and get gas. We pull up to a rundown gas station that doesn't even have a name anymore because the sign fell off. Julian slips out of the car and begins to fill up the gas tank.

"So, why exactly are we going to Los Angeles?" Nash wonders from the back seat.

"Leslie called me and said she was at a warehouse in L.A."

"Is that all she told you?" Nash began. I look back at Nash and he looks genuinely concerned.

"Yeah, the call dropped."

Julian goes inside the gas station to pay and comes back out a couple minutes later, handing me Coconut Berry Juice.

"No way! They have Coconut Berry Juice here?" I blurt, slurping down the juice after ripping the cap off.

Nash laughs. "What is that?"

I gasp. "You've never had it from the Surf Shack?"

He grabs the juice out of my hands and drinks from it. Nash just drank from my cup. I think I'm going to die because Nash's saliva is all over my cup. It sounds nasty if you think about it like that, but it's Nash's saliva so I don't even care.

"That's good," Nash admits.

I'm glad he likes it. If he didn't like it, I would no longer like him. Okay, that's a lie. But, still, my future husband needs to like Coconut Berry Juice or it wouldn't be a very happy marriage.

I take the juice back from Nash. "Yeah, I know, but it's mine."

Julian starts the car and we pull away from the gas station and onto the freeway. I unbuckle and climb over the seat into the back of the car so that I can sit next to Nash. He looks at me and smiles. We talk about what kind of music we like and our favorite foods the rest of the car ride. Thankfully, he likes the same kind of music that I like.

Julian drives the car into a rest area and says, "Look at Google Maps so we can find all of the Wellmington warehouses in L.A."

Twenty minutes later, the station wagon skids into the parking lot of the first warehouse we had decided to check. As we're pulling into the parking lot, I look out the window at the warehouse. The outside of it has light metal paneling, from which the sunlight reflects off of it. It's a tall building, probably the equivalent to four stories.

"Jeez, Julian, slow down," I yell, falling into Nash's lap.

The three of us get out of the car and head over to the giant sliding doors. With one strong pull, Julian and Nash pry them open and we sneak in.

"Is this illegal?" Nash wonders, looking up at the rows and rows of shelves that fill the warehouse.

Of course I know that breaking and entering is illegal, but the doors were unlocked, so technically we didn't break into anything; we just entered. I guess that still means we're trespassing, but it's not illegal if we don't get caught.

I slide a box off of one of the shelves that is labeled 'Coconut Berry Juice' after searching the warehouse for a what seemed like an hour.

"Oh my gosh!" I shout.

"What'd you find?" Julian and Nash hurry over to me from another aisle.

"It's the recipe for Coconut Berry Juice," I squeal in excitement. I've always wanted the recipe for Coconut Berry Juice. I even tried to bribe the manager of the Surf Shack for the recipe last year, but he said it was a priceless secret. I shove the recipe into my pocket and start dancing around.

"Are you serious? I thought it was something important," Julian grumbles.

Nash starts laughing at my bad dance moves, so I stop dancing and give him a dirty look. We search almost a hundred boxes in the warehouse, but there are no clues as to where Leslie could be.

"Well, that was a waste of time," Nash states, getting into the car. I get into the back seat of the car with him.

"It wasn't a complete waste of time; I got the recipe."

He chuckles at my obsession with Coconut Berry Juice. I swear all Nash does is laugh at me. Is that a good or bad thing? I'm not really sure.

Forty-five minutes later, the car comes to a sudden stop.

"The warehouse is right over there. It doesn't have a parking lot," Julian says, climbing out of the car.

Nash and I follow Julian over to the entrance of the building. The exterior of this building looks almost identical to the last one. However, the doors on this warehouse are already wide open, and the interior of this building is different; it has no shelves and is completely empty.

"What's that?" I point to an odd looking painting of the sea that's on the wall by the door.

"Whoever painted that must've been high," Julian jokes. I move the painting off of the wall. There is a drawing etched into the metal; it's a ten-point star. A star with water dripping off of the bottom right point of it.

I stare at the star blankly, and then I smile. "She was here. Leslie was here."

The star is a symbol my mom taught Leslie and me. When we were younger, my mom would go out while we were sleeping, and she'd always leave a picture of a star with water dripping from it. Apparently it means 'Nepos Strong'.

Julian and Nash both look at me with surprised expressions on their faces.

"Where do you think she went?" Nash wonders.

Julian and I both shrug our shoulders, not knowing what to say. We search around the rest of the warehouse thinking we might find another clue, but we don't find anything. Not even some dust.

By the time we walk out of the warehouse and into the car, it is already nine at night. Right when Julian starts the engine, it starts down pouring.

"I can't see anything through the windshield," Julian hisses ten minutes later.

The rain has only gotten worse since we left the warehouse, and Julian isn't exaggerating. I can't see a single thing through the windshield except water. I am tempted to try and move the water away, but then I remember Nash is in the car with us.

I'm glad that Nash came with us, but I wish he knew what I really am. I look over at him and he's sleeping. How could he be sleeping right now? The rain is so loud I can barely even hear myself think. I climb up into the passenger seat.

"Let's try to move the water."

Julian glances back at Nash, then gives me a nod, and we both focus on the water. The water begins to move off of the windshield and pour onto the road around us. The rain starts to come down in bigger drops and hits the windshield even harder than before.

"It's not working," Julian remarks. I check up on Nash to make sure he's still sleeping, but he isn't; he's staring at me in astonishment.

"What did you just do?" he asks, dumbfounded.

"It's just a dream. Go back to sleep," I soothe.

Nash lays his head down on the side of the car door and falls back asleep.

"That was close," Julian whispers.

I roll my eyes. "Yeah, I know."

"Maybe we should just stop at a hotel around here. It's going to take forever to get home now," Julian suggests. I give Julian an agreeing nod and he takes an exit off the highway. I want to turn on my rock music and blast it really loud, but I don't. Nash looks so cute when he sleeps; I just can't turn the music on and wake him up.

After a while of riding in the car in silence, we pull into a rundown looking motel.

"Nash, wake up," I whisper before getting out of the car.

"Huh?" Nash rubs his eyes in a tired voice.

I am absolutely obsessed with a guy's sleepy voice. Especially Nash's. It sounds so perfect.

We make our way into the motel and Julian rents a suite for the night. We get a suite on the third floor and head into the elevator. I never thought I would admit this, but it's a good thing Leslie isn't here right now; she's deathly afraid of elevators.

Julian swipes the key and the suite door unlocks. I push open the door and hop onto the first bed.

I look around the room, noticing how uncomfortable it is in here. The walls are white metal, but they seem to be pretty old. As for the flooring, it is silver metal, and it appears to be shinier than the walls. When I finish taking the appearance of the small room in, I realize that there are only two beds in here. Where is Nash supposed to sleep?

After a while of discussing it, we decided that Nash gets his own bed, and Julian and I will share a bed. It sounds a little strange, Julian and I sharing a bed, but it's really not that strange. Julian and I have known each other since we were five. Julian, Leslie, and I met at the morgue the day we all had to identify our parent's bodies. The day I met Julian was one of the worst days of my life, but it was also one of the best days of my life because I made a lifelong friendship that day.

I take my shirt off, forgetting Nash is in the room. When I'm at home with Julian and Leslie I sometimes sleep in just my sports bra and jeans, so I'm used to it.

"Oh, sorry," I sputter because I see Nash staring at me. I pull a blanket over myself and lie down on the bed.

Nash chuckles and switches the light off. Did he seriously just laugh again? What's so funny about me embarrassing myself all the time? I just don't get it.

I hear Julian start to snore, and the sound of him snoring puts me right to sleep.

CHAPTER 9

Rollercoaster

I hear the sound of a toilet flushing and open my eyes. Nash is standing in front of my bed putting his pants on over his green briefs. I almost scream. He turns around and sees me staring at him.

"Good morning." He grins from cheek to cheek. Julian walks out of the bathroom brushing his teeth.

"Where'd you get that toothbrush?" I ask as I yawn.

"It was in a bag somebody left in the bathroom," Julian admits.

"That's disgusting," I groan, getting off of the bed. I don't even care if Nash sees me in my sports bra anymore. I mean, he already did last night. I pick my shirt up off of the floor and throw it on over my head. Nash looks away, but I can tell he's watching me out of the corner of his eye.

I go into the bathroom and close the door behind me. I turn on the faucet and make a ball of water float into the air in front of my face. I splash the ball of water onto my face to wake me up.

"Okay, I'm ready to go," I state, coming out of the bathroom a few minutes later.

Nash smiles while putting on someone else's deodorant, and, oddly enough, he looks good putting it on. Oh, who am I kidding? He looks good no matter what he's doing.

"One second. I can't find my car keys," Julian says, digging through the blankets of the bed we slept on.

It's been almost ten minutes and Julian still hasn't found his car keys.

"Maybe you should go ask the motel manager if you left your keys down there last night," I suggest.

"Okay, good idea," Julian says before sliding out the door.

Nash and I are in the room alone. I know we've been together this whole time with Julian, but it's different being alone with just Nash. When I'm alone with him I get more nervous to talk. I don't see any reason to be nervous though. I mean, he's seen me in my sports bra.

"Do you think the car keys will be down there?" he asks, sitting down next to me on the bed.

"Hopefully," I mumble, scooting farther away from him.

He scoots closer to me and whispers, "I don't bite."

I laugh, even though it's not funny. I absolutely hate it when people say that they don't bite. I just want to scream that I know he doesn't bite. But I don't, because it's Nash, and I still like him, despite him saying that he doesn't bite.

I scoot farther away from him and accidentally fall off of the bed and onto the floor. My body hits the ground and I can feel a bruise forming on my thigh.

"Ow," I grumble.

"Are you okay?" Nash peaks over from the top of the bed. He stretches his arm out to help me stand up, but instead of pulling myself up, I yank him onto the floor next to me. He starts laughing so hard I think his eyes are going to pop out of his head. It isn't that funny, but I start laughing too. I can't help it.

He grabs a pillow from the bed and hits me in the head with it. If it wasn't a feather pillow, I would be really mad. I pick the pillow up off of the floor and hit Nash with it in the stomach really hard.

"Take that." I snort, gasping for air. After about a minute of hitting each other with pillows, we both give up and just lie on the floor trying to catch our breath.

"Well, that was unexpected," Nash says.

I look over at him and he is smiling really big. I've never seen him smile this big before.

"Tell me about it."

Nash and I frown at each other, because we hear yelling coming from downstairs.

"What was that?"

"I don't know. We should probably go check it out," he insists.

We shoot into the hallway and I press the elevator button. The elevator makes a dinging noise and we get in.

I press the button for the first floor and the elevator slams downward while playing a classical song that sounds like something my mom used to listen to. I don't remember much about my mom, except that she liked classical music and braiding my hair.

Nash starts to sway his hips to the music, but before I can even laugh at him, the elevator jolts to a stop, the doors remaining closed.

"Are we seriously stuck?" I ask, annoyed.

"I think so." He clicks the help button on the panel.

"Now I know why Leslie's afraid of elevators," I announce, tapping my foot nervously.

"Sorry, we're unable to help you at this time," the speaker in the top right of the elevator blasts.

"Uh, excuse me?" I hit the help button about ten more times, before it gets jammed stuck. Well, this is great. Now it's just replaying the word 'sorry' over and over.

Nash begins trying to pry the doors open, but they won't budge. Which is surprising because he has huge biceps. Believe me.

Twenty minutes have already passed, when the light in the elevator flickers off.

Nash grabs my hand and says, "I got you. Don't worry."

I never told him that I was scared, but, oh, well, he's holding my hand, and that's all that matters to me. Wait, Nash is holding my hand? He's holding my hand and I didn't even ask him to. I'm not even scared anymore; I think I'm going to faint from excitement.

I was about to say, "I wasn't even scared," when the elevator drops. I lose my stomach; it feels like I'm going down a hill on a tall rollercoaster. Thankfully, it doesn't drop to the ground, it just drops to the first story.

I breathe a sigh of relief. The elevator dings and the doors open. I have no idea how the elevator got fixed, because there are no maintenance people around. In fact, I don't see any people at all.

We sneak up next to the main lobby desk, following the sound of the shouting. I try to run over to the people who are yelling, but Nash grabs my arm and pulls me back behind the counter.

"Listen," he says out of the corner of his mouth. There are two people arguing about Leslie; one of them sounds exactly like Julian.

"Is that Julian?" I ask.

I peek my head over the top of the desk after the shouting stops and see him standing there with a huge laceration in his chest. I blink a few times to make sure I'm not hallucinating.

"Julian, are you okay?" I sprint over to him as fast as I can.

He falls onto the floor. "She was here. Leslie was here."

Nash and I exchange confused glances. I unzip my purse and pull out the sparkly green scarf that I bring everywhere. I like to be prepared: you never know when you'll need a tourniquet or run into a disco party with nothing to wear. I wrap the scarf around Julian's bleeding wound and pull it tight.

He points towards the glass door, and I see the man in the trench coat throwing Leslie into the back of a white van. My heart stops at the sight of Leslie. Her skin looks more pale than usual, and I can see bruises on her legs as he throws her in.

I bust out of the motel door, and chase the van for about five seconds, before it's out of my vision, and there's nothing I can do to stop it. I feel so terrible thinking about what Leslie could be going through right now. If only I had super speed instead of hydrokinesis.

I hurry back into the motel to see Julian and Nash waiting for me, sitting in the fluffy blue lobby chairs.

"Did you get the license plate?" Julian tries to stand up, but sits back down in pain.

"It was N-0-H-A-T-3." I plop into the chair next to Nash.

"That's ironic," Julian announces, but stops smiling when he notices Nash and I aren't laughing.

Julian's wound starts to bleed through the scarf. I gag at the scent of the oozing blood creeping its way into my nose. The scent of blood always makes me feel nauseous.

"We need to take you to a hospital," I dictate.

I pull my iPhone 31 out of my purse and search for the nearest hospital. I know what you're thinking, and, no, the iPhone 31 isn't the size of a baking pan. Phones have actually gotten a lot smaller in the past few years. The iPhone 31 is about the size of a small Roku player remote.

"The closest hospital is fifteen minutes away." We carry Julian out into the motel parking lot, and Julian swipes his keys out of his pants pocket. I stare at the keys blankly.

"Where'd you find them?"

"They were in my pocket the whole time."

I laugh and roll my eyes. He hands them to Nash. Sadly, I still don't have my license, so Nash has to drive to the hospital.

After a little less than fifteen minutes in the car, we swerve into the Red Cross Emergency parking lot. Nash and I put our arms around Julian and help him slide out of the car. The two of us prop him up and bring him into the hospital waiting room. Sitting down, Julian falls off of the couch ten seconds later, and passes out on the grimy white tile floor. I stare at Julian; I don't know what to do.

Is he going to be okay? Am I going to lose yet another person in my life? I cringe at the thought. My mom was a nurse, but I never wanted her to teach me anything.

"I need some help out here," the scrawny lady behind the computer yells down the emergency hallway.

I sway my head up, away from Julian, and see two doctors running over to us with a stretcher. The doctors sweep Julian up off of the ground and lay him down on the yellow gurney.

Nash and I start to follow the doctors into the long, crowded hallway, but one of the doctors motions us away. "Stay in the waiting room."

Nash and I walk over to the couch and sit back down. Neither of us talks to the other while waiting to hear from the doctors; we're too worried about Julian right now to form a sentence.

The silence is interrupted by the lady behind the computer. "Anything I can get for you?"

"Oh, no. Thanks," I answer, scooting off the couch and onto the floor.

"Why are you on the floor?" Nash asks from above me.

"I don't feel like sitting on the couch anymore."

To be honest, I just got off of the couch because of how uncomfortable it is. It's about as comfortable as a pile of rocks on fire.

"I'm not good enough for you?" he jokes.

I ignore him, because I get distracted by a blue sticky note underneath the couch. I scrape the sticky note off of the leg of the couch and pounce up next to Nash.

"Look at this." I read the words aloud, "Griffith Park. 6 p.m."

"Griffith Park? We passed that on our way here," he recalls.

How did Vincent know we'd be sitting on this exact couch in the hospital? I try to ignore the super creepy thought and put the sticky note into my pocket. Vincent seems to know everything.

Twenty-five minutes pass before a doctor comes out of the hallway and informs us that Julian had to get stitches. He'll be fine.

"Can we see him now?" I wonder.

"Yes." The doctor heads back down the hallway, and we follow behind him. Julian's room is the last room in the entire hallway: Room 157. We walk into the room, and the doctor leaves, shutting the door behind him.

"Hey, Julian," I whisper, standing above him. He moves his arms, prying himself up.

"The doctor said I can leave in an hour."

"Why an hour?" Nash wonders.

Julian shrugs his shoulders, picking up a Styrofoam cup of water from the bedside table. He tries to take a sip of the water, so I use my mind to splash the water in his face. I can't help myself.

Nash's jaw drops open. "How did you do that?"

I completely forgot Nash doesn't know about us. My bad.

"I guess I'm a little shaky," Julian answers, throwing me an evil glare. I always fail to remember how easy it is to expose our secret.

I change the subject as fast as I possibly can. "So, how much do the stitches cost?"

"The doctor told me the bill has already been taken care of," Julian reports.

"Did you pay?" I nudge Nash.

"No."

The three of us are bantering about who could have paid the bill, when the doctor bursts through the door.

"You can leave now," he insists.

We all head out of the door, down the hallway, and into the waiting room. I walk over to the lady behind the computer.

"Who paid our bill?" I ask.

"A man in a long coat. He said he was your father," the lady answers.

Julian, Nash, and I head out of the hospital, and jump into the station wagon. I tell them who paid our bill, and I also show Julian the sticky note from underneath the couch.

"Speaking of the note, what time is it?" Nash wonders.

"Five forty-five," Julian answers.

It will take us about fifteen minutes to drive to Griffith Park. Perfect.

CHAPTER 10

Classic

The engine booms as Julian starts the car, and we are off. I blast One Direction on the radio as loud as it can go, because I kind of miss it. Julian and I start to sing all of the lyrics to the first song, when I notice Nash in the back of the car, looking at us like we're lunatics. I giggle to myself, because I realize I'm acting exactly like Leslie. By the time four songs are over with, we drive into Griffith Park's parking lot, and we all slump out of the car.

"I thought it was a park, not a museum," I say while observing the building.

"I guess not," Julian responds as we walk up to the entrance.

Nash points to a sign on the door. "It says the building closes at five."

I tug on the door handle, and it's unlocked. We sneak into the museum, trespassing once again, and the first thing that I see is a large dinosaur skeleton. Classic.

I poke at one of the toe bones on the dinosaur. "Do you think there are security cameras in here?"

"Most likely," Nash answers.

I sigh. I really want to take one of the bones from the dinosaur. The reason I want to take a bone is because our mom left us a bag of animal bones in her will. I know that it was just a strange hobby of hers, but I want to add to the collection.

I'm thinking about how epic it would be to own a dinosaur bone, when the museum doors behind us slam shut.

"Uh, who did that?" I croak.

Nash looks around everywhere in confusion. "We're not scared of you."

"I am," Julian makes known, trying to hide behind me.

I spin my head around, and the man is walking right towards us. He breathes heavily and steps out of the shadows, to reveal that he is carrying Leslie. She is lying in his arms, sleeping. At least, I hope she's sleeping. My eyes widen as I look at Leslie's bruises once again. She opens her eyes and tries to say something, but she can't, because of the duct tape that is across her lips.

"Mr. Wellmington?" Nash questions.

I can tell he's figuring the whole thing out, just by his expression.

"Don't even think about hurting her," I growl, clenching my fists.

The man sets Leslie down onto the tile floor and kicks her side. She can't even move; she's all tied up in ropes.

"What do you want from us?" Julian's voice echoes throughout the whole museum.

"I'm just having a little fun," the man snickers evilly.

Nash stands in front of me and bellows. "We know what you are."

The man laughs in a creepy deep tone. Actually, it wasn't even creepy, it was just plain weird.

Wait, hold on. What does Nash mean '*we* know what you are'?

I don't have time to ask; Leslie is just lying there. Pushing past Nash, I sprint towards her. I reach down to untie her, but the man is standing above me, laughing. A rope is in my grasp, but something isn't right, the rope won't budge. As I handle another piece of the rope, I feel an electric shock go through my whole body, causing me to black out.

CHAPTER 11

Shadowstrike

I open my eyes and hear nothing. No noise. I look around to see that I'm in a tiny white room, with no windows and no corners; it's a completely round room with only a gray door and a mail slot on the bottom of it. I reach for my phone in my back pocket, but my pocket is empty. This isn't good.

There's a faint knock on the door.

"Hello?" I croak.

A tray slides through the mail slot, and I hear someone's footsteps walk away from the door. I sit up and crawl over to the plate of food. The tray has cheesy mashed potatoes and a green apple sitting on it. I reluctantly pick up the apple and take a huge bite out of it. Mm. It actually tastes pretty good. I finish the rest of the apple and throw the whole tray through the mail slot. I decide not to eat the mashed potatoes, because, obviously, I hate mashed potatoes. Who likes them, anyway?

The tray comes flying back through the mail slot with a blue sticky note stuck to the side of it: Eat the potatoes.

"I don't like mashed potatoes," I yell out to no one.

The door handle unlocks and a guy wearing a ski mask busts the door wide open. He shuts the door behind him and locks it.

"Eat the potatoes."

"Is that mask supposed to scare me?" I ask.

He growls and pulls a pistol from underneath his shirt. But this isn't just any pistol. It's a Shadowstrike: the pistol the Praetor who work for King Praetor carry around everywhere. I always thought it was a myth, but I guess it's not.

"Jeez, chill. They're just potatoes."

"Eat!" the guy demands, pointing the pistol at my head. I shove my mouth full with the mashed potatoes, trying not to vomit from the taste. He lowers the pistol and goes back out of the room, locking the door.

I open the mail slot and peek out of it. I can see two pairs of shoes a couple of feet away from me. One pair is Leslie's blue flip flops. My heart starts racing and I swallow a clump of saliva to keep myself from screaming for Leslie. I've finally found her, and I still can't do anything to help her.

I stick my ear up to the mail slot and listen. I can barely hear what they're saying, but I can make some of the words out.

"I don't wanna be on your side," Leslie stomps her feet, causing the flip flops to make a clapping noise.

"You don't have a choice. You know your dad is a Praetor," the guy wearing the ski mask's voice echoes.

What does he mean Leslie's dad was a Praetor? He couldn't have been a Praetor. Nepos and Praetor are forbidden to have children. It's not possible that Victoria told me the truth, is it? Is Vincent really Leslie's dad? Oh, no, this can't be happening. This would make Leslie half Nepos, half Praetor. This is bad. Very bad.

"I know my dad was a Praetor, but that doesn't mean I *like* the Praetor."

"You're half Praetor, my dear," someone states as he enters the room. His voice sounds familiar. It's definitely Vincent.

"I don't care!" Leslie tries to run, but Vincent knocks her over, and drags her by her ankles. Leslie's body skids right next to the mail slot. Her eyes are wide open, staring right at me. I stare back at her with a frightened look written on my face.

She's getting dragged away from me when I hear Vincent throw her into a room and slam the door. If my hearing is correct, then she is in the room right next to mine, and Vincent is in there with her.

I scoot to the middle of the small, white room and start to think. *How did I get in this mess? What happened before I was in this room?*

Then I remember; the long rope that Leslie was tied up in earlier electrocuted me and knocked me out. I can almost feel the shock again as I think about it. It felt like a bunch of tiny needles were flying through all of my limbs. I don't know if I've ever physically felt that much pain before. The rope must have been a Venom Grasp: the weapon that was often used by the Praetor during the war.

Ten minutes have passed by when he finally decides to leave. I make sure that he's gone, and slide over to the right wall of my room. I knock on the wall, and a second later, I get a knock back. My heart pounds rapidly and I can feel it in my feet, my head, and even at my fingertips.

"Leslie?" I whisper-yell through the wall.

"Andy?" Leslie answers.

"We need to get out of here."

Just then, the guy with the ski mask bursts into my room, or should I say, 'Jail cell'?

"I heard talking," the guy shouts.

I stare at him with a dirty look, until he gives up on me and leaves my cell. That always works, just give someone a dirty look, and it makes them uncomfortable enough that they'll eventually leave you alone.

I peer out of the mail slot to make sure that the ski mask guy is gone, and he is.

Leslie and I chat for a while, trying to think of a plan to get out of here, but we come up with nothing. I am starting to fall asleep leaning against the wall, but, right before I'm about to doze off, the guy with the ski mask comes back through the door.

Trying to annoy him, I say, "you look taller."

"Let's get out of here," the guy suggests.

"Huh?" I inquire, standing up. The guy sighs loudly and rips off his ski mask; it's Julian.

"Julian!" I run over and tackle him, almost knocking him over.

Julian shushes me and we sneak over to the room that Leslie's being held in. Julian pulls a ring of keys out of his pocket, and searches for the one that has B2 engraved on it. They really are like cells. The rooms have numbers and everything. We bust into Leslie's cell and she looks up at us in surprise.

"Come on," I urge. Leslie jumps up, and we all scramble out of the room.

This feels good: the three of us being together again. It's amazing. I knew we'd find Leslie at some point, I was determined to find her. But I never thought the three of us being together again would feel this great. Especially considering we're in a prison that looks like something that you'd see in a horror movie. There are blood splatters all over the metal floor and everything.

After a few seconds of walking, I notice Julian and Leslie aren't next to me anymore. I look behind me and see them amorously hugging each other. Oh, great. I'm already the third wheel again. I run back over to them and tell them to hurry up.

We're walking down a slim hallway, when we soon learn we have to make a decision. On the left, a path leads into another small hallway. On the right, a large, but dim lit hallway sits. Either we turn left, right, or we can always choose to keep going straight.

I turn to my left and ask Julian, "Which way?"

"Left. I think we should go left."

"Okay, come on."

The three of us turn into the hallway and see nothing but doors. Doors everywhere. They're short, wide doors, with black paint that is peeling off on each of them. We continue trying to find our way out of this hallway for over five minutes, when I see a significantly taller door with a sign above it that reads 'staff only'.

"Guys." I point to the large doors.

"We can't go in there, Andy. We're trying to escape, not get caught." Leslie hugs me. "I'm glad to see you, I really am. But that's a terrible idea."

"I think we should go in there," Julian adds, nodding at me.

"Whoa, did Julian Garcia just ignore a wish made by Leslie?" I ask.

The three of us chuckle silently. I lead the way over to the doors. I push one open a crack, and luckily, there's no one on the other side.

"Come on," I whisper, motioning for them to follow me. I slide my body through the crack of the door, trying not to open it too far.

Once all of us have made it into the disturbingly cold room, my eyes widen with fear; the room has machinery everywhere. But that's not the terrifying part; there are masks of skin hanging from the ceiling. Not just a few either: thousands. The skins are suspended on clothing hangers, as if they're waiting for someone to put them on. Though I'm far below the nearest skin, I can see the veins and intricate detail put into these body masks. Each mask looks as if it was just taken off of someone's living body.

"You guys. This is disgusting," Leslie says from my left.

"This must be where the disguises for the Praetor are created." I gulp. "Guys, we're in King Praetor's laboratory right now."

"Wouldn't that make Vincent . . .," Leslie begins.

"King Praetor? Yeah, it would."

Since Vincent is King Praetor, that means Leslie is a princess. Is that why he wanted her back in his family? So she could be an heir to his throne? But what about Victoria? Leslie isn't even full Praetor; Victoria is. It's all starting to piece together, though. I now know why the Wellmington's own a bunch of warehouses. The warehouses are where they create their freakishly accurate disguises.

"We need to get out of here, now," Julian says, fear in his eyes.

As I begin to push open the door, I hear someone coming from the other side. My brain overloads with worries as I hear talking getting closer and closer to us. I see a tall, metal counter nearby and I scurry over to it. With Julian and Leslie beside me, we all duck behind the massive chunk of metal, wishing for the best. Hearing someone walk through the door, I slowly peak my head around the corner of the counter. I see two men in white lab coats, heading towards a mask of skin that is lying on a table. They begin poking it with a scalpel and smiling at each other.

"This sample is in perfect condition. It's ready for her to wear it," one of the men says, wiping a bit of blood onto his coat.

Looking at Julian and Leslie, I bite my own lip, keeping myself from whimpering with fear. I can tell they're doing the same, too. After a few seconds have passed, the men finally make their way out of the room.

"We're leaving. Now." I bust through the door, not caring if anyone is on the other side. I'm getting out of here. The image of those skins hanging, I'll never forget.

Minutes later, as I'm fast-walking, I find myself stumble upon an exit sign. I don't know if it's really an exit, but if it is, I'm so glad that I found it. I honestly don't even care about being trapped at this point. I just want to get out because Leslie will not stop talking about how she lied; she doesn't like anyone else and she only loves Julian.

I open the door in glory, but it isn't so glorious after all. There are two tall, lean guys in black ski masks standing there, both holding an enormous Shadowstrike. They hold up their guns and try to make us go back inside of the warehouse.

I nudge Julian in the shoulder, nodding towards the pond full of water near the side of the building. Julian, Leslie, and I put our hands in the air like we're going to surrender and the men start screaming in a different language, which just sounds like random noises to me.

"Are your weapons waterproof?" I give Julian and Leslie a nod, and the three of us use all of our strength, lifting the water out of the pond and into midair. I use the last ounce of energy inside of me and force the water downward, dumping the entire pond onto the guys' heads.

I see the men, or, most likely, Praetor, both take hard falls onto the grass. The water washes back down the hill and into the pond trench, leaving the masked guys lying on the wet muddy grass. I smile to myself. I knew our powers would come in handy at some point.

"Come on," Nash hollers, running up to us with the car keys in his hand. Everything around me starts to get blurry.

"Guys, wait." I fall onto the mushy green grass.

CHAPTER 12

I'm Up for a Little Snack

"Andy, please, get up," Nash begs sitting against a wall.

I stretch as I sit up. I'm in the back of a van.

"What happened?" I ask.

"You've been out for a day. Before we got separated, Leslie said Mr. Wellmington most likely drugged your mashed potatoes."

Oh. That's why that guy in the ski mask was obsessed with the potatoes. I look around, not seeing Julian or Leslie with us.

"Where did they take Julian and Leslie?"

"I'm not sure. Mr. Wellmington put them in a different car," Nash murmurs, "I think he's King Praetor."

I slide over to the other side of the car, next to Nash.

"Yeah, he is. But how do you know about the Praetor?" I ask, confused.

"I'm a Medicus."

My pulse starts rising. Medicus? That's impossible; they've been extinct for five years now. "That makes no sense."

"My family is the last of the Medicus."

"Why didn't you heal the cut in Julian's chest then?"

"I wasn't sure if you were Nepos at the time," Nash admits.

"Oh."

Medicus are the species that the Praetor had a war with because the Praetor didn't want the Medicus healing the Nepos anymore. The Praetor started the war so they could capture and harvest all of the Nepos without the Medicus to help us. A Medicus can heal a Nepos of anything, a cut, a bruise, even cancer. But, if a Medicus tries to heal a human, they'll both die, so I guess what Nash is saying kind of makes sense. I have a thousand more questions for him, but I figure asking them won't change anything. Plus, I'm still a little loopy from the drugged potatoes, and my head aches from thinking so much.

Hardly any time passes when the van stops with a loud thud. Nash and I stare at each other, trying to guess what's going on.

The back of the van opens, and the man is standing in front of us in his black trench coat. He ducks into the overly large white van and comes over to me, smiling. He has blood running down his chin. This is dreadful. Utterly dreadful. If he tries to drink my blood, I'm not sure what I'll do in defense.

He lifts me up by the collar of my Mickey Mouse t-shirt. He starts to run his fingers up and down my throat. I gulp, staring straight into his eyes, trying to be strong.

"I'm up for a little snack."

Nash rams into Vincent, making him drop me and leaving him speechless. Nash lifts me up over his shoulders and lurches out of the van.

He sets me down and I start sprinting as fast as my legs will carry me. I can't stand the thought of Vincent drinking my blood. It just makes me think of how my mother died. I glance behind me and see that Nash has almost caught up with me. Not far behind him is Vincent.

"Hurry!" I call back to Nash.

We're in the middle of nowhere. Everything around us is brown, dusty dirt. I have no idea where we're going to run, but it's the only option we have.

Nash darts up next to me, and we keep running in sync for what feels like fifteen minutes before we see a neglected house in the distance. A lot of houses were destroyed in the war, but this looks to be one of the only houses that's still made out of wood.

The humans thought it was just a war about racism because a Praetor has porcelain white skin, while a Medicus is more on the tan side. Silly, oblivious humans. Almost every single building in California has been rebuilt, and now everything's made with silver, steel metal to protect the buildings from bombs.

We dash up to the moldy yellow house and kick the front door open. I jump up onto the crumbly rotting stairs that lead up to the second story, Nash following. I swoosh down the hallway and push through the second to last door.

"There," Nash exclaims, pointing to a bed with a gun pattern all over it.

Oh, how grand. We're in a redneck's house. I hope he isn't one of those crazies that will shoot our heads off and feed us to his pet pigs. And then eat the pigs for dinner tomorrow.

We drop down onto the light wood floor and slither underneath the bed. All I can hear is Nash panting into my ear because we were running for so long. Nash's breath is super warm. Ew. I give Nash a 'be quiet' glance, and he covers his mouth with his hand.

Right when I think we have lost Vincent, the wood paneling creaks downstairs.

"Did you hear that?" I whisper.

"Yes." Nash puts a finger up to his lips and hushes me.

The stairs make an earsplitting noise, and I begin to panic. He's getting closer. Nash drags a knit blanket from the side of the bed and piles it onto our bodies. This blanket is way too itchy for my liking, but if it saves my life, then I can deal with it.

I'm side by side with Nash right now, hiding under a blanket, in a redneck's house. Well, I definitely didn't think this was the way we'd spend our first time under a blanket together.

"Oh, Andrea . . . I know you're in here," Vincent barks from the hallway. He steps into the room, "Come out, kitty kitty."

I don't know what's happening because I can't see anything from underneath this blanket. It's pitch black, scorching hot, and I can barely breathe without choking on my own breath. I began to cough and I feel Nash's hand cover my mouth.

I hear footsteps march out of the room. A small gleam of light comes in from the side of the blanket as Nash peeks his head out. He rips the blanket off of us and slides out from underneath the bed.

"There," he says, pointing to a window leading to a roof balcony.

I scrunch out from under the bed and tiptoe over to the window. Nash unlatches the locks and jerks open the window. I crawl out, following Nash's lead. I'm not sure how we're going to get onto the ground from the second story.

I peer over the gate to see a beaten up pavilion beneath the balcony. Nash sees it at the same time as I do and tells me to get onto it first. Without hesitation, I climb over the top of the gate and onto the roof of the pavilion.

"Ugh." I land onto a pile of vines covering the entire roof. I leap off of the pavilion and onto the concrete.

Nash jumps onto the pavilion, and, to my surprise, it doesn't collapse. I'm not saying that Nash is fat or anything, but he weighs a lot more than me. I mean, his muscles are so big, he could pick me up with two fingers.

Nash's feet smack down onto the concrete next to me. "Let's get out of here."

CHAPTER 13

Lifesaver

We've been jogging for twenty minutes, and there is no sign of any living animal or bug species in the entire area. The only thing here is a forest full of pine trees.

"Maybe we should go into the woods. The road isn't doing us any good," Nash says, slowing down into a steady walk.

"I don't know," I debate, slowing down next to him. Nash starts leading the way into the woods, but we turn around to the sound of a swooshing car: a white van.

"No hate," Nash announces, reading the front license plate. I'm just catching my breath, and now I have to run, again.

We duck behind some bushes and wait for the van to pass us. I race after the car as fast as I can and try to jump onto the back of it, but I miss. Nash bolts past me and springs onto the back of the van, clutching onto one of the two handles.

"Come on," he says, stretching one of his arms out.

This is it, I have to make it this time. I gather up all of the strength in my body and dart. I hurdle onto the van and shift my weight up with Nash's help. I grasp the other handle with my right hand and throw Nash a smile. It's a good thing there's a little ledge on the back of the van, or we'd be toast.

The wind is blowing my hair around like crazy; I feel like I'm riding on a dune buggy. I grab onto Nash's body so I won't fly off, and turn the handle. The door flies wide open.

Nash and I dive into the back of the van. Ow. That really hurt my hip. But I don't have time to think about my hip. I look up and Julian and Leslie are staring at us. I smile at the sight of the two of them. I really missed them. I know it has only been a day since I've seen them, but to me it feels more like ten years.

I hold one of the van doors halfway open so I can see where we are and prevent us from getting locked inside. We all scoot over to the other side of the van and get caught up on what's been happening.

Nothing exciting had really happened to Julian and Leslie. They just sat in this van for hours and hours. When Nash and I told them about the house, and how we've been wandering around, they were jealous. It seems stupid for them to be jealous at us being lost, but I suppose anything is better than sitting in a van for over twenty-four hours.

After an hour of catching up and talking about how Vincent is dumb for wearing a trench coat in the heat of California all of the time, I see something; we're driving into a city.

"Guys, look." I point to a sign with the word 'Irvine' written on it. Irvine is a city a little less than half an hour away from Laguna Beach.

The van comes to a halt. We're in a traffic jam.

"Let's go," Julian demands.

I push the door open the rest of the way. All four of us jump out of the back of the van, and a bunch of cars honk angrily at us. We slide our bodies in between the cramped cars and eventually make it onto the metal sidewalk.

"Uh, oh," Leslie croaks, pointing towards the van.

The driver, who is wearing a ski mask, plops out of the car and looks right at us. He can't do that. He can't just leave his car in the middle of a traffic jam. The guy starts charging towards the four of us.

"Go, go, go!" I holler.

I'm so tired of running; it's not even funny. We start sprinting towards a shop called 'Sweet Treats'. From the looks of it, it's a candy store. Julian forces the pink door forward and we all scurry into the shop. The boy behind the cash register with the nametag 'Henry' stares at us.

"Take all of the candy you want, I don't have any money," he proposes, holding out a lollipop.

"Thanks. But we're not here to rob you," I answer, before changing my mind and snatching the lollipop out of his hand.

Leslie nudges me in the shoulder and hisses, "You can't just take the lollipop."

"He offered," I scoff, licking the lollipop.

I see Nash smiling at me out of the corner of my eye. I always knew I was funny. I just had no one to appreciate my humor until now.

"What are you doing here?" Henry interrogates, flipping his long orange hair.

Before any of us can answer him, the guy with the ski mask busts through the door. Henry frowns, looking at the guy's mask.

"This one has to be robbing me."

"That's why we're here," Nash informs him.

We all dash into the back storage room of the candy shop, leaving Henry behind. I look around. There are at least thirty racks full of candy.

"This is Heaven," Julian states. He seizes a handful of starburst out of a large bucket.

"Oh, and I couldn't have one lollipop?" I respond.

My eyes dart around the room, looking for somewhere to hide, but I find something even better than a hiding place.

I almost scream. There's a blue fridge full of Coconut Berry Juice. I start bouncing up and down excitedly.

"Look, guys."

"Whoa, I didn't see that," Leslie admits, walking over to a door.

Oh, there is a door next to the fridge full of juice. I guess that's a lifesaver too. Everyone heads out the door, but I don't. I need at least one bottle of Coconut Berry Juice before I can leave.

I open the fridge and pull a bottle out. "My love."

"What are you doing? Get out here," Leslie yells and I join them outside.

I know I should be scared right now, but I'm not. I have my favorite drink in the world in my hands. I twist the cap off of the juice and take a big gulp. Leslie scowls at me, eying the drink. Nash swooshes the drink out of my hands and takes a sip.

"I like it." He winks.

I'm not positive if that was supposed to be funny or creepy, so I just laugh, and take the juice back from him. There is a loud thunderous crash from inside the candy store, and I take another gulp of the juice before shooting Julian a frightened expression.

"Let's go. Now," Julian orders.

After running as far as our bodies will allow, we start to wander around on the sidewalk for a while, hoping that the guy won't find the back door. I really missed this: walking around on the busy streets of California. It puts me at ease.

CHAPTER 14

Crinkly Bag

I step onto the gazebo and sit down on the bench of a clean, white picnic table. We wandered around for a good twenty minutes before we got out of the streets and found this nice, quiet park. Leslie's stomach grumbles.

"I haven't eaten in forever," she complains.

"None of us has," I shoot back.

"What's that then?" Julian chimes in, pointing at my juice.

"Uh, it's a drink. Not food."

Why do they always have to team up on me?

Nash taps me on the shoulder and shows me a vending machine straight across from the gazebo. The vending machine would be way more exciting if Vincent hadn't emptied all of our pockets.

"I don't have any money."

Nash walks over to the vending machine and starts to shake it like crazy. He returns to the gazebo along with four miniature bags of Chips Ahoy in his hands. He sets the cookies down on the picnic table and we all snatch our own bag of them.

"Oh my gosh. I love you," I sigh, as I rip open my bag of chocolate chip cookies. Oh, no, I just said I love him. I didn't mean it like that. I was just excited about the food.

Nash smiles and shoves his face with a stack of cookies. I swing my head to the side and see Julian feeding Leslie a cookie. Trust me, I missed Leslie, and I'd do anything for her, but why can't she just eat her cookies like a normal person?

Julian picks up a cookie and nibbles on it, like a mouse nibbles on a piece of cheese. Actually, I don't know if mice even eat cheese. I think that's just a myth.

Okay. I'm aware that Julian and Leslie are my best friends, but they're being really annoying right now. They just are. I can't explain it, but if you knew them, you'd understand.

I am thinking about how they are being more annoying now than they usually are on the ride to school, when a thought comes to my attention and I ask, "Where's the station wagon?"

"Crap." Julian coughs on a piece of his cookie, probably because he was eating it like a mouse. But, anyway, we sort of need the car back, or we'll be stuck here because we don't have any money to ride the bus.

"We don't have our phones either," Leslie adds.

"Yeah, I know. I haven't been on Tweeker in forever," I snarl.

By the way, Tweeker is the social network that is cool right now. I especially like it because I get to see what all of the hottest stars are doing on the daily.

Everyone starts laughing at me. I have no idea why they're laughing. Ugh. Why do I always have to get laughed at? I pull a cookie out of the bag and bite into it.

"It's not funny that I have no clue what my favorite celebrities are doing right now."

They all laugh even harder this time. What did I say? It's not my fault I miss reading tweeks. Jeez.

I dig into the crinkly bag for another cookie, but they're all gone. Aw, dang it. I'm still starving. I lean over towards the trashcan and throw my empty wrapper into the trash. Everyone copies me and throws their wrappers away too.

Nash and I are strolling behind Julian and Leslie; I don't want to walk next to them when they're being love birds. We chat for a while and agree to head back towards Laguna Beach. Vincent could easily find us there, but we both just really miss our beach. Right now, we're not worried about him finding us; we just want to get home.

"Start walking home. West," I shout up to Julian and Leslie, because I don't feel like running all the way up to them.

Leslie turns around and scowls, "That's too far away."

"We'll get there eventually," I hear Julian say, and Leslie shifts her body back around.

CHAPTER 15

Reality Check

It's beginning to get dark and the bugs are coming out. Gross.

I don't know what the time is because the idiot, Vincent, took my phone away from me. Vincent thinks he's so clever, with his trench coat and his dark black eyes that remind me of cow manure. Whatever. I don't have time to think about him right now. I need to focus on getting home.

I kick a pebble as Nash and I catch up with Julian and Leslie. We have to make it home tonight. Not only because I want to snuggle with a warm fuzzy blanket on the couch, but also because we don't have any money and we could starve to death.

The four us are strolling along the road, side by side, determined to get home. For the first time, I'm actually not the third wheel.

Even though I should be scared or frightened that we can't get home, I'm not at all. It feels great, all of us being together. For some reason, I'm happy.

I stop walking mid-step, swing my head upward, and just stare at the stars for a moment. There they are. The two stars that are shaped like diamonds. After my mom died, Leslie told me that she imagined that one of these stars is my mom watching over us. I don't believe her; I think it's a stupid theory that the star could be our mom. If you ask me, there's no such thing as afterlife. But Leslie believes it, she believes that one of the diamond stars is my mom. In fact, she says she knows it is.

Somehow, seeing the stars give me a reality check. I know we have to settle down somewhere for the night, and we'll figure out what to do tomorrow morning.

I draw my head away from the sky and realize everyone else is staring up at the stars too. I wonder what they're all looking at, considering Leslie is the only one who believes in the star theory. The three of them bring their heads down from the stars and look at me. It's kind of intimidating, all of them staring at me.

I shift my feet and begin to start walking again. I don't know where we're going to sleep tonight, but we need to find somewhere. Somewhere that doesn't cost any money.

"Let's find somewhere to stay the night," I suggest. Actually I didn't really suggest anything. It was more like I demanded it. Luckily, all of them nod their heads in agreement.

We glide our feet in rhythm, not saying much, except the occasional, "I'm tired." I'm pretty sure—no, I'm 100% positive that each of us has had our fair share of complaining about how tired we are right now.

After a very long time of sliding my sneakers alongside the paved road, I see a sign in the near distance. I move my legs as quickly as possible to reach the sign faster. Finally, I'm close enough to read it. The sign reads, 'Ridge Trailer Park.'

I walk past the sign and around a corner of hedges. There it is, a huge park full of abandoned trailer homes. I motion the gang over to where I'm standing, so they can see the homes too.

They hurry over, Leslie riding on Julian's shoulders. She hops off of his shoulders and frowns at me.

"You want us to sleep in one of these crappy shacks?" She looks as if she is going to puke.

I just hope she doesn't vomit on my shoes. Julian got me these sneakers for my birthday a few months ago, when I turned sixteen. Before I got these shoes, I only owned a pair of broken orange flip flops that I've had since I was five.

Julian pats Leslie on the head like she's a dog. "It'll have to do." He looks disappointed in my lack of finding a safe place to stay the night.

To my surprise, Nash doesn't say anything about the situation.

I can barely see anything, including myself. I scoot closer to what looks like a trailer, but I honestly can't tell. I run my fingers on the side. Yup, it's definitely siding. I haven't felt siding in a long time, because most buildings are metal now. I slide my hand along the wall until it bumps into the door handle. I grasp the handle, and it feels like no one has touched it in years, which is probably true. Turning the handle, I hear a noise behind me; it sounds like some type of rodent running around.

"I think I just saw a mouse," I whisper.

I hate rodents, they gross me out. I continue opening the door; it's good thing it's unlocked. As I push open the door it squeaks so loud, it probably wakes all of the rodents up. I hope it didn't.

I tiptoe into the home, and feel the wall for a light switch, but no luck. What kind of house doesn't have any lights? I walk forward into the darkness, the floor creaking with every step.

"Ow," I say, aloud. Something dangling from the ceiling just hit me on the head, and I have no idea what it is.

I hear Julian, Leslie, and Nash ask, "What?" from behind me, but I don't feel like answering.

I put my arm up and reach around for what I had hit my head on. What I feel in my palm is way more exciting than it should be. It's a beaded string, a beaded string connected to a light bulb. I pull the string down and a bright flash of light blinds me. I look behind me and all three of my friends are standing there shielding their eyes.

"Sorry, I should've warned you guys."

"No kidding," Leslie retorts, uncovering her eyes. Julian slowly takes his hands away from his face and looks around at the room.

"This is revolting," he grumbles. Nash looks at me and shrugs his shoulders, in agreement with Julian.

I scramble over to a plaid couch, and sadly, find out it's not a pull out couch. Thankfully, there are two long couches, and one short one. Julian and Leslie bounce onto one of the long couches, and begin to cuddle.

Man, I wish I had what Julian and Leslie have. I get onto the short couch, and let Nash have the other long couch. Even though we're all extremely tired, we decide to talk for a while. Nash isn't really talking much, so I look over at him and notice that he's already sleeping.

Oh, that's why he wasn't talking, I think, lying my head down against a very uncomfortable pillow. Before I know it, Julian and Leslie are sound asleep too. I guess it's time for me to go to bed.

CHAPTER 16

Halfway Through Puberty

I chuck an old ratty pillow off of my lap.

"Ugh. It's so hot," I complain.

Nobody responds to my complaint, so I look around and they're all still sleeping. For the first time in a long time, I'm the first one awake.

I glide over to the fridge and open it. Nothing. The fridge is completely empty. Well, I guess it does make sense, considering this place has been abandoned for who-knows-how-long.

I shut the fridge and open the cupboard above the empty space where there's supposed to be an oven. Nope. Nothing in the cupboard either. I slam the cupboard on accident and wake Nash. He gets up off of the couch and stretches for a very long time.

"Morning," he says, walking over to me.

There it is again, his sleepy voice. I try not to freak out over how adorable his sleepy voice is, but I can't help it. My eyes widen and my face turns completely red. That's what happens when I try to hold my excitement inside.

Nash looks at me with a strange face.

"Does that mean morning back?" he asks.

I smile and give him a big thumbs-up because I can't find the words to say. Somehow, he always manages to make me smile. Even at the bad times, like right now, not having any food. I suppose it's not the worst scenario, not having food, but whatever.

I open a drawer below the uninstalled sink. Hmm. There's one knife in the drawer. Just one, nothing else. I slide my hand around, trying to feel for anything other than the useless knife.

"Ow!" I yelp, feeling the blade slice through my skin. The palm of my hand starts oozing blood, not nearly as bad as Julian's cut in his chest was, but pretty close. Okay. It's not even close at all.

Nash walks over to me and holds my hand. I stare into his eyes, and the pain in my palm instantly feels numbed. He looks away from my hand and up into my eyes. This is the moment I've been waiting for. The moment where he should kiss me. This is it.

He yanks his hand away from mine.

"Your cut should be fine now," he says, turning and walking away.

I glance at my hand and it's completely healed, with no scar. *Wow. How did he do that?* I've never met a Medicus before Nash.

I look up at him. Why did he turn away from me so quickly? Is something wrong?

I'm just about to ask if he's ok, when Julian twitches, and Leslie falls off of the couch. Leslie stands up and holds her head in pain.

"Really, Julian?" She hits him in the side.

Julian stands up off and stares at Leslie angrily.

"Yes, really," he groans.

I'm not trying to be mean, but Julian's sleepy voice isn't cute at all. He sounds like a boy halfway through puberty. His voice cracks non-stop when he first wakes up.

I hold it in, trying not to laugh at how ridiculous his voice sounds right now. I rarely get to hear his sleepy voice, since I always wake up after him.

Julian and Leslie apologize to each other, and start hugging. Ugh. Stop hugging; it's not fair.

Nash turns around and looks at me with a depressed face. I want to ask him what's going on with him, but I don't want to push our boundaries. Besides, it probably has nothing to do with me.

"So, are we going home now?" Julian asks, walking towards me.

I nod my head. "We'll make it as far as we can."

I'm about to open the door, but something catches my eye: sunlight is reflected from behind the couch. I walk over to the couch and reach behind it. What I feel in my grip definitely isn't what I expect. It's my phone.

Julian, Leslie, and Nash, stare at me with blank expressions on their faces. I click the 'on' button, and it's already on.

This is impossible. I haven't had my phone with me the whole time since the warehouse incident. I check the dialed and the missed calls: no new calls. I check the text messages;

there's a text message in the draft section: *You won't make it home.*

I show the message on the screen to all three of my friends. We look at each other in confusion.

"Someone was here while we were sleeping," Leslie whispers.

I want to say, "No kidding," but I stop myself. I don't feel like making Leslie mad right now.

Julian nods his head in a frightened manner.

If someone was here while we were asleep, how did Leslie not wake up? She's the lightest sleeper I know. If someone drops a Nerd — the candy, not an actual nerd — onto the floor, she will wake up. Last year I got up in the middle of the night to sneak some chocolate out of the cupboard, and Leslie woke up before my feet hit the ground.

Moving on, I pretend I never saw the text message and shove my phone into my back pocket.

"Why didn't they bring my phone?" Julian whines.

In a way, I don't really care about the message; I got my phone back and now I can catch up on my tweeks.

Nash still doesn't say anything, which is a little concerning. I open the door and everyone follows me out of the trailer. We walk out of the trailer park and begin walking on the side of the road. Something splatters on my head. I feel the top of my head with my hand, and it's bird poop.

"Ew!" I screech. I'm acting like Leslie right now, but I don't care. It's bird poop. Get it off of my head right now.

Nash turns around and takes his shirt off. Wow. He looks good. He starts wiping my hair with his shirt, in an attempt to get the poop off of me. He swipes the bird poop off of my hand and tucks the shirt in his back pocket. Ew. The poop is in his back pocket.

I can still feel the bird poop residue in my hair. This is possibly the grossest thing I've ever been through. Now I have another reason to get home: to take a shower. I haven't taken a shower in forever. I feel absolutely nasty.

A car flies by us and sprays me with a puddle of mud. Are you kidding me right now? Now I need to take a shower even more than I did before. I didn't think that was possible. Nash laughs and throws his shirt at me. I wipe myself off as good as can, and throw it back to him. It's nice to see him smile again.

I kind of feel bad for ruining his shirt. Oh, who am I kidding? I don't feel bad. I can't feel bad. I mean, he looks so good without it. His abs are harder than rock. Actually, I don't know if they are; I'm just guessing. I hope they're harder than rock; that would be amazing.

We turn onto another road that is extremely busy. Cars keep flying by us non-stop. I make sure to stay farther away from the road, to avoid getting sprayed by more mud.

"Seriously?" Leslie pouts, stepping into a rain puddle.

When did it rain? I don't remember it raining. It barely ever rains here. The last time it rained was last weekend, and that was the first time in a long time.

Julian sweeps Leslie off of her feet and carries her. Of course, Leslie gets to be carried because her feet are wet, and I just get wiped off with a bird-poop-covered-t-shirt. I'm not trying to complain about the t-shirt, though. I just don't like how Leslie always gets everything she wants. Well, not everything. I guess it would've sucked to be her when she got kidnapped. But other than that, she gets everything she wants.

Last night we walked for an hour and a half, which means, in walking distance, we still have two and a half hours left to walk. That's just wonderful. I can't walk two and a half hours without quitting, especially because all I've eaten in the past two days is a miniature bag of Chips Ahoy.

CHAPTER 17

Orange Scruff

We've been walking for almost an hour now. I can't take this any longer. My legs are sore, my back hurts, and I'm really sweaty. And, might I say, I hate being sweaty. It feels like I'm taking a shower, except in my own sweat. I swear, it's boiling outside, and I think I'm starting to hallucinate.

I'm annoyed with my own thoughts when a low humming noise catches my attention. I look behind me, and a beat-up orange truck is slowly levitating towards us.

The levitating truck is the first flying automobile so far. It's an epic failure, too. It looks like a floating pile of junk.

I see that Julian, Nash, and Leslie, all have odd expressions on their faces. The truck pulls up next to Julian, in the front of our pack. The passenger side window inches down, squeaking as it goes.

"You kids need a ride?" says a woman with a little bit of orange scruff on her chin as she sticks her head out of the window.

I'm not trying to be judgmental or anything, but from the looks of her, she's not very trustworthy. I mean, I might trust her a tad bit more if she had shaved her beard.

Julian takes two steps away from the truck.

"No, thanks," he says with a disgusted look written all over his face.

I knew I wasn't the only one who was judging this lady. Julian always says he doesn't judge people, which definitely isn't true, because everybody judges people.

The truck doesn't move.

"Let me rephrase that: Get in the car," the bearded lady says as she raises her voice.

By this time, Leslie's face is dripping with fear. Literally. She's sweating bullets. Leslie always sweats when she scared. I don't see why she's afraid, other than the beard. It's just a creepy lady with a beard. If you live in California, you'll see ladies with beards all the time.

The lady creaks open the passenger side door and scrambles out. Wow. She's way bigger than I thought she was, and I was now getting a better look at her face. She has large blue eye bags underneath her eyes, along with a hairy brown mole smack dab in the middle of her chin.

She gropes my arm, and looks me straight in the eyes. "Do you wanna go home or not?"

Okay, now I know why Leslie's scared. I start grinding my teeth back and forth in nervousness.

"I'm fine walking," I choke, trying to avoid eye contact.

Nash yanks the lady's hand off of my arm.

"Get lost," he growls.

Up until now, I don't think I've ever seen Nash be rude. Which is strange, considering he's one of the most popular guys at school.

I see Julian holding Leslie in fear. Julian may be tall and slightly buff, but he's not being much of a man right now.

The lady snickers and hops back into the passenger seat. She whispers something to the driver. He just looks like a dark figure from over here. The driver hands her two small objects. The lady holds her hand out of the window. She's holding Julian and Leslie's phones.

Leslie runs up to her hand and tries to grab her phone.

"My baby! I missed you," she screams excitedly, losing all of her fear.

"Hey, what about me?" Julian snaps, running over to get his phone too.

I can't believe they're risking their lives to get their phones back. Well, I guess I probably would too. But luckily, I already have my phone back, safely in my pocket. I reach into my pocket just to make sure it's still in there; I never know what to expect anymore. Phew. I still have it.

When Leslie tries to grab her phone for the second time, the lady grasps Leslie's arm. Why is it always the arm with this lady? Does she have an arm fetish or something? She pulls Leslie forward. She's surprisingly strong. Leslie's only around 110 pounds, but, still, this lady looks like she has no muscles whatsoever.

The lady breathes heavily towards Leslie. I can see Leslie cringe from the smell of her breath. I know why, too; I can smell the lady's breath from six feet away. Apparently, she was just eating garlic bread, with extra garlic. That's repulsing. I detest garlic bread. Every time I eat it, I end up throwing it up ten minutes later.

Julian smacks the lady's hand and she lets go of Leslie's arm, dropping the phones onto the blistering concrete. Julian and Leslie snatch up their phones and back away, next to Nash and I. The lady's face turns bright red in anger.

"You rotten kids!" she growls.

"Excuse me; I'm sixteen," I sass back to her.

I find the best thing to do when you're scared of someone is to pretend you're not. I suppose it didn't work with Vincent all too well, though. I don't know this lady's name, so I'm just going to call her Bobby Jean, because it sounds like a hillbilly name.

Bobby Jean grimaces. Oh, of course. She has a ton of missing teeth. How did I miss that before? Her teeth are all yellow and covered in scum. Somebody, please, get me a barf bag, now. I'm not saying that people can't be different than me, but, please, at least brush your teeth — or in this case, tooth. Please, brush your tooth.

Bobby Jean opens her mouth and begins to speak, "I told you to get in the car."

I'm so confused right now. Why does she have a southern accent if she's in California? Anyway, I see what looks to be a leftover chunk of food stuck on her tooth. Yes. I totally called that. I guess I should try to focus on what she's saying and not on her appearance.

"Do you want me to get out of the truck again?" she threatens.

Leslie looks like she's going to pee herself, and Julian's hands are trembling like he has epilepsy. Nash is standing next to me, with no emotion on his face. I hope I don't look as frightened as Leslie does right now.

Bobby Jean whispers to the dark shadowy driver, again. The driver hops out of the truck and walks around the side of the car. He looks at us with a strange look on his face. He's taller than Julian, which is super tall. I swear, he's about the size of a skyscraper. He has dark toned skin, and is wearing a navy blue button up shirt, with tan khakis. If he's trying to be scary, it's not working. Well, it was until I noticed the khakis. He doesn't have any facial hair, which is weird because Bobby Jean has facial hair. The one who you would expect to have facial hair doesn't.

He steps closer to us, "I'm De'Andre," he states in a voice that sounds exactly like the guy from the old Allstate commercials.

"I'm guessing you used to be a basketball player," I say.

Leslie looks at me and shakes her head. I hear Nash trying to hold in his laugh; he sounds like a dying seal.

"Don't be stereotypical!" Leslie snaps at me. Julian nods his head in agreement with Leslie.

De'Andre chuckles, "I used to play college basketball."

I'm surprised. He seems way kinder than Bobby Jean. Leslie has a snotty look on her face. Ha. I'm actually right for once. De'Andre walks even closer to us.

"Would you like a lift?"

"We said, 'No, thank you,'" Nash states from beside me.

I notice that Nash is breathing heavily. Hey, maybe he actually is scared for once.

Even though De'Andre seems nice, I'm still nervous. My mom always told me that the sneakiest kidnappers are the nicest. I think about the story my mom used to tell me all the time. She would say: *There once was a little girl. She called herself Penelope. She was a sweet girl, filled with joy. But one day, there was a guy. He was dressed in a dark red jacket, and he wore gladiator glasses everywhere he went. He was an African American; he had skin like a dark chocolate chip. The guy saw Penelope at her school and asked her if she needed a friend. She said, "Yes." The guy and Penelope hung out every day after school, without her parents knowing. Two years went by of them hanging out, and Penelope was now ten years old. Penelope and the guy's friendship started to fade as she got older. On October 31, 2006, Penelope was found dead in a dumpster behind an Olive Garden. The guy still hasn't been caught for the murder of Penelope. He's hiding in the shadows.*

I imagine my mom's light tender voice saying it to me. I remember it word for word. I always hated that story; it used to scare the crap out of me; it still does.

What if De'Andre is the guy? He fits the description perfectly. Although, he'd be almost sixty years old now. This guy looks like he's in his mid-thirties.

De'Andre doesn't say anything in response to Nash's comment; he just stares at us with a blank look on his face. My hands start to tremble; it feels like there are ants eating away at my skin. The story of Penelope runs through my mind over and over. I really don't want to end up like her.

We've been walking long enough that we're not in the city anymore; there's nowhere to hide. It's just my luck that this happens right now. Why couldn't this have happened when we were still in Irvine?

I begin to move my feet, leaving my friends behind. I'm running so fast I feel like a cheetah who just had some catnip. I don't know where I'm going; it's just paved road for miles. I need to get away. The Penelope story won't get out of my head. I feel like all I've been doing lately is running away. I really need to stop running away from my problems; it's a bad habit.

I've only been running for a few seconds, and I'm already out of breath. I turn around, and see Nash, Julian, and Leslie, being shoved into the tiny back seat of the truck.

"No!" I shout in anger. I suddenly feel my eyes start to swell up with tears. I'm all alone.

The truck's engine rumbles from behind me. I turn back towards the truck. My legs feel like Jell-O because I'm trying to run, but I'm barely moving. I should've never left without my friends.

I gather the ounce of strength I have left in me, and start sprinting towards the truck. I'm doing it. I'm running. I keep both of my eyes on the truck to make sure it doesn't move. I feel something beneath my feet; it's a huge chunk of ripped up gravel. I'm going so fast. I can't stop, and I trip, sweating bullets.

I scramble my body up, and feel a sharp pain in my knee. I look down and it's oozing thick red blood. There are chunks of miniature rocks stuck inside my cut. I begin to run, but it's too hard. I fall onto my knee again, causing even more pain.

CHAPTER 18

Focus

I hear the roar of the truck's engine getting closer. I'm unable to move; I'm too weak. My leg bones feel like wet noodles.

I swing my head up from the pavement and see a fuzzy image of the truck heading straight towards me. I feel someone swoop me off of the ground and throw me into the truck carelessly. From the feel of the manly hands, it's probably Bobby Jean. I feel the entire car shift in the air. Do I really weigh that much?

I glance over at Nash, Julian, and Leslie. We're all so squished together; it feels like we're being stuffed into one little sleeping bag. Leslie's next to me. I can tell she's trying really hard not to look scared. From the look of Julian, he's not trying very hard. Nash has a curious look on his face. I wonder what he's thinking about.

The pain in my knee gets worse. It's starting to gush out even more. Nash looks at my knee and hesitates whether or not to help. He reaches over Julian and Leslie, and puts his palm on my knee. I feel my knee glide shut. The feeling of wounds shutting like that is a feeling I wish wasn't real.

Nash lifts his hand away, and it's covered in my blood. Ew.

I have blood dripping down my leg, but my knee is completely healed. I still find it strange that Nash is a Medicus. Somehow, it makes me feel uneasy about him. I can't deny the attraction between us, though. I still have a huge crush on him, and I probably always will.

Nash wipes my blood off on his shorts. He can't wipe it off on his shirt because he's still not wearing a shirt. Ha.

I crack a smile at Nash, trying to hide my pain. He smiles back. The truck floats up higher into the air, and the radio blasts on at maximum volume.

Bobby Jean turns on the car radio and a popular country song comes on. She begins to sing along with it and bob her head.

I see Julian lip-synching along with the music as well. I give him a dirty look.

"Have you been secretly listening to country?" I whisper-ask.

Julian squirms, trying to get out of the uncomfortable position we're all in.

"Psh. No," he says.

I can tell he's lying. When does Julian even have time alone to listen to country music? Leslie begins to say something but gets interrupted by Bobby Jean.

"No talking!" Bobby looks back at us, yelling from the front seat.

I roll my eyes. Just because we're in her stupid truck, doesn't mean we have to listen to her.

I untangle my body and re-adjust.

"Hey, Bobby." I tap her on the shoulder.

Bobby looks back at me, with a mean look on his face. I mean her face. I keep forgetting she's a girl.

"My name's Eugene," she growls.

Eugene is an even worse name than Bobby. I laugh, and Bobby — er —Eugene, glares at me with a look almost as evil as one of Victoria's.

I slump into my seat, to avoid making Eugene even more upset. Everything that's happened over the past few days rushes through my mind. Dang. We've all been held hostage a lot lately. But this time it feels different; I feel like they're actually trying to help us. I mean, they aren't wearing ski masks. That's a good sign, right?

I pull my mind out of the gutter and try to focus on how to get out of this. My body feels warm and sticky; covered in sweat. I see the sweat glimmering on Leslie's body next to me. She's trembling uncontrollably.

"Are you okay?" I whisper to her.

"I'm fine," she sighs.

De'Andre shifts in his seat in front of Nash.

"Can you not talk?" he asks. Suddenly, his deep friendly voice disappears.

Julian starts laughing really hard. "He sounds like a white girl."

Nash starts chuckling along with Julian. Leslie rolls her eyes, because she talks just like that. I contain my laughter for as long as I can but, before I know it, I'm laughing with the boys.

The truck comes to a halt and bounces in the air. I hate being in a levitating car. It makes me nauseous.

"We said, 'No talking!'" Eugene yells.

All four of us look at each other with surprised expressions on our faces. Julian pretends to zip his lips, throwing a fake key out of the window. Somehow, Julian's nervousness has gone away. He's more calm than me. Although, I'm not very calm. I'm just acting like it.

The truck starts driving again, so I lay my head down on the side of the window.

I doze off for fifteen minutes, when I wake up to the sound of pouring water. I look around the truck; everyone's sleeping. I peek into the front of the car, Eugene and De'Andre are gone. They're nowhere to be seen.

I hear the sound of the water pounding around me. I peer my head out the right window, and then the left window; the truck is hovering a good fifteen feet above the peak of a rushing waterfall.

"Guys, get up!" I scream, pushing on Leslie's shoulder.

Leslie rubs her eyes and mumbles something that I can't understand. Nash and Julian open their eyes in confusion. All three widen their eyes at the same time, hearing the water falling around us.

Soon, I realize that the levitation gauge, next to the gas gauge, is running very low.

"We need to get out of here," I yell. I can hardly hear myself over the noise of the pounding water.

"What is it?" Leslie hits my left shoulder.

"The gauge. We only have a minute left."

"What gauge?" Julian asks, holding onto Leslie's hand.

"The levitation gauge, Julian. Gosh," I growl, "Now come on. Help me do this."

I hold my palm facing outward to the waterfall.

"Andy, we can't do this. It takes too much power," Leslie whines.

"Yes, we can. Just trust me."

Julian and Leslie hesitate, but hold their palms outward, too.

"One, two, three."

The three of us clench our fists, focusing all of our energy on the water.

The water from the river begins to move upwards slowly, but starts to get pushed back down stream by the current. I swallow a hard ball of saliva, trying to keep myself in focus. I look back at the gauge; it reads half a minute. When I glance back at Nash, he gives me a reassuring nod. We have to do this. If we don't, we're going to die. I don't want to die. I don't want them to die. A large gust of wind flies by me, causing water to pelt me in the face.

"Keep going," I tell Julian and Leslie.

We put our palms out once again, and I close my eyes, feeling the water hit me in the face. I ignore the rapid pain, and focus every inch of energy inside of me on the falling water. We lift our palms upward, and the water starts to join together in a large clump, rising upwards. I feel the mass of water hit the bottom of the truck, and the truck bounces a bit from the sudden jolt of pressure.

I throw Julian and Leslie a look, telling them to help me move the water to the side of the waterfall, where the grass is. They nod, and I begin to target the center of the water beneath the truck with my mind. I feel the truck start to move to the right, beneath my feet. We start moving slower, and slower, but I keep my mind focused on getting to land.

"Focus, Leslie," I demand.

Leslie rolls her eyes and looks back towards the water splashing her in the face. I look at the time, we have two seconds and we're still at least a foot away from land. We don't have enough time to make it. My legs start shaking and I'm sweating everywhere, despite the fact that I'm covered in freezing water.

"Jump!" I scream as loud as possible. I lunge for the grass and I hit the ground, my knees throbbing in immense pain. I bury my head in the hands, kneeling in the grass. I can hear the truck hit the large rocks at the bottom of the waterfall and I cringe at the sound. That could've been us.

I look to the right side of me, where I see Julian and Leslie hugging each other while crouched on the ground. I turn around and crawl to the ledge of the water. I start panicking, and my palms begin to get sweaty. I don't see Nash anywhere.

"Where's Nash?" I scream.

Before Julian or Leslie can answer me, I hear a voice.

"Andy!" Nash yells.

I peek over the edge and see Nash hanging onto the slippery wet, muddy grass. His legs are being swung around by the falling water and being hit by pebbles.

Without thinking, I reach my hand over and grab Nash's left hand. I try pulling him up, but I don't have enough strength. I feel Julian come up behind me and I sigh in relief. Julian extends his arm to Nash's other hand. I look at Julian and he nods. We pull up Nash as fast as we can, and he slides up onto the grass. Julian and I fall backwards onto the grass from pulling so hard.

Nash lies on the ground beside me on his back, breathing really loud. I scoot over closer to Nash and lay my head on his chest.

"We did it," I say. The wind flows through my hair and I feel alive. Completely and utterly alive.

I gather myself up slowly into a sitting position, ignoring the pain in my bones. Julian and Leslie crawl over towards Nash and me, and we all sit together.

I breathe a sigh of relief; we're all still here. We're all still alive.

CHAPTER 19

It's a Long Story

All of our faces are covered in dried mud, and our hair is super greasy. I can tell everybody else is getting fatigued, too. The last time we've eaten was . . . yesterday? Or the day before? I'm not even sure anymore.

My feet tremble; we're getting closer to home. I'm beginning to recognize some of the buildings that are surrounding me. At this point, I'm so tired that I could lie down and go to bed right here on the scorching metal sidewalk.

We probably should have stayed somewhere after the whole near-death-experience with the waterfall, but I'm more determined to get home now than I ever was before.

"Ugh. What time is it?" Leslie complains from behind me. She pulls out her phone and checks the clock.

Thinking about phones makes me wonder whatever happened to Nash's phone, but then I realize it's in the back pocket of his shorts. Nash sees me staring at his butt and laughs.

"See something you like?" he asks, grinning.

"Oh, sorry. I was looking at your phone." My face turns red with embarrassment. I thought I was done being afraid to talk to Nash, but apparently I'm not.

"It's 4:27," Leslie chimes in.

I decide not to say anything in response; she does know I have my phone too, right?

Nash taps on my shoulder. "Can I talk to you for a sec?"

Leslie gives me a smirk, indicating that I should go with him.

"We'll wait over here," she says, pulling Julian away from Nash and me.

I nod at her and shrug, wondering what Nash could possibly want to talk to me about. I follow him just a few feet away from where Leslie watches us intently. We stand on a small grass patch, and I wait for him to say something. After waiting a few long seconds for him to talk, I break the silence.

"So, what do you need to talk about?"

"Listen, Andrea, I really like you." He looks at the ground. "But I need to tell you something."

My eyes fixate themselves onto his. I stare into his eyes, pressuring him into what he so desperately needs to tell me.

"Go ahead."

"The thing is. . ." He kicks the grass, and a large chunk of dirt breaks from the ground. "Vincent sort of, maybe, thinks I'm working for him. I've been using my phone to communicate with him."

Feeling my veins intensifying with confusion and anger, I contain myself, waiting for him to explain further.

Nash gulps. "The only reason I ever dated Victoria was to get closer to her family. My family, being Medicus, needed to know more information on how the Praetor work. How they disguise themselves, how their minds work. You know, the basics.

"After dating Victoria for a few months, Vincent found out I was Medicus. He then thought he could blackmail me into helping him find some Nepos. So I pretended to search for him, hoping to get more information for my family."

He itches his arm nervously and continues, "When our road trip first started, I was texting Vincent. I was giving him subtle, inaccurate, hints as to where we were. He really wanted you and Leslie. Why? I don't know. But, listen to me, I never would've let him hurt you."

Releasing a bit of the tension, I answer, "Are you kidding me right now, Nash? The reason you came to find Leslie was to help Vincent? Not to help me?"

"I never wanted to help him. I wanted to help my family. My family wants to get rid of the Praetor for good. We'll win this time."

"I'm not a fan of war, Nash. And, to be honest, I'm not a fan of you right now, either."

Dang. You might as well call me The Sass Master. Slowly, I begin to calm myself down. Though I don't like Nash in this moment, I understand his reasoning.

"Are you the one who put the sticky note under the couch in the hospital?"

"Well, yes. But I only put that one there to prove to Vincent that I was loyal. But I'm not, though. Not to him, at least. I'm sorry. I really am."

"Whatever. I guess I forgive you and everything."

With a sudden memory, I say, "But wait, you said you didn't heal Julian because you didn't know if he was Nepos or not. Since you were working with Vincent, you should've already known we are both Nepos."

"You didn't know I was Medicus. And, if Vincent found out I healed Julian, he wouldn't trust me anymore."

Being as annoyed as I am right now, I hardly even realize what Nash has said to me. He said he liked me. Like, a lot. Plus, he's a double agent, and that's really hot.

Nash sighs and puts his hand on my shoulder.

"Promise you forgive me?" he asks.

"I promise."

After kicking the small patch of dirt that Nash had earlier broken apart, I head back towards Julian and Leslie. Leslie smiles at me, her face still smeared with a bit of mud.

"So, what happened?" she grins.

"I'll explain later."

"Come on, tell us. Did he finally admit he likes you?" Julian says as Nash begins to approach us.

"I mean, kind of. But I'll explain it later."

Over half an hour later, I drag my feet along the sidewalk, more tired than ever before. I look around at the neighborhood; it's kind of sad what it looks like. I should be used to it by now, since I grew up like this, but I'm not. The buildings are all covered in thick shiny metal. By the time I'm ready to call it a day, Nash's face lights up.

"What is it?" I ask, sweat dripping down my face.

"Over there, it's Leon's car! I recognize it by the license plate," Nash exclaims.

Leon is one of Nash's best friends, although I never understood why. He has scruffy dark brown hair and dresses like he lives in a dumpster. He's also one of the most popular guys in school, which still makes no sense to me.

Leslie looks at me with both excitement and disgust. I'm not sure which to feel either. Should I be excited or disgusted?

The four of us scurry over into the Beach Bum's restaurant parking lot.

"We should go inside. It'll look suspicious if we stand out here by his Mercedes Benz," Julian suggests.

I nod in agreement with Julian. Nash grabs the handle of the door and holds it open for Julian, Leslie, and me.

A lady jumps in front of us and snaps a picture, and the flash is so bright, I almost faint. I look around at the restaurant, my eyes still foggy from the flash. What I see is very odd. All of the walls are covered with pictures of the customers. Which is pretty creepy, if you ask me. It's unique, though, and I have to admit, it's also kind of cool.

"Hi. How many?" a hostess with a high knotted bun asks as she walks up to us.

"Uh, well —," I begin.

Nash looks back at me with an 'I got this' look on his face. "Four," he says.

Julian and Leslie look confused, too. At least I'm not the only one left hanging like the skins in the warehouse. Okay, bad reference. But you know what I mean.

We follow the waitress over to four empty bar stools. I hop onto one of the stools with Leslie on my right side, and Nash on my left. Julian is, of course, on the other stool next to Leslie.

"Hey, isn't that Leon?" I point over to a dining table a few feet away from us.

"Yeah, he's with Landon." Nash squints his eyes to make sure it's them.

Landon is Leon's twin brother. They're basically exactly the same, except Landon dresses nicer and has clean hair. Leon sees us staring at him and hops out of his chair, running over to Nash.

"Nashie Boy! Where have you been all weekend?" Leon barks obnoxiously. Landon follows behind Leon, looking like a lost puppy. Their faces alone give me a headache.

"It's a long story," Nash sighs.

Leon looks at me with a blank look on his face. "And who are you?"

"I'm Andrea. We've gone to school together since preschool," I hiss.

"Oh. Yeah, that's right, Andrea," Landon says from behind Leon.

Leslie plops off of her stool and stands beside mine. "I'm Leslie, Andrea's sister," she pipes.

Leon chuckles and runs his fingers through his distractingly greasy hair. He doesn't have an excuse for his hair being greasy; at least we do.

"And who's the Mexican?" Leon responds to Leslie.

"I'm Julian. I've also gone to school with you since preschool," Julian snarls holding his hand out.

Leon hesitantly shakes Julian's hand and wipes it off on his pants.

Nash spins around in his stool, making it squeak super loud.

"So, can we get a ride home?" he urges.

Leon and Landon debate about it for a few minutes, until they finally say in harmony, "Fine."

"Thanks, guys." Nash pats each of them on the back.

I don't like seeing Nash with his friends; he acts different, more immature, or something. I guess everyone acts more immature around their friends, though. I mean, how else would we be able to have fun?

"Wait one second; I gotta grab my keys," Leon says as he walks back over to his table.

He returns holding his keys in one hand and a piece of steak in the other.

"All right, let's go," he mumbles, shoving the rest of a steak into his mouth.

The four of us, well five, if you count Landon, follow behind Leon until we reach the parking lot once again. Leon hops into the driver's seat, and Landon hops into the passenger seat.

I stare at the Benz, there are only three seats in the back. Three. We're going to have to be squashed together again? I think I've had enough of that for one weekend.

As Julian, Leslie, and I are getting into the back of the car, I see Nash scrambling around in the front. He's pulling up another seat in the middle of Leon and Landon.

"You sit here, Andy." Nash looks at me and pats the center of the seat.

I sigh in frustration while hopping into the front, switching seats with Nash.

"You're the smallest," Leon winks at me.

Ugh. Gross. Did he just hit on me in some sort of creepy 'Leon' way?

I try to ignore the fact that I'm sitting between the twins I've been disgusted by ever since I was a little girl, but I can't. I keep seeing Leon scratch his greasy hair and sniff his hand as if there's a scent to dandruff. I look over at Landon, in an effort to ignore Leon's stupidity. What I see him doing is a huge surprise, I never thought I would see one of the twins doing what he's doing. Landon is reading a book. A book. A book called 'The Novel of Abraham Lincoln'. I can't believe what I'm seeing.

After a while of staring at Landon in disbelief, I realize how quiet the ride has been so far. Is it because I'm sitting in the front? Probably. Ugh. Maybe I'm just thinking too much.

I begin to glare at the digital clock below the CD slot, willing the time to go faster so I can be home. Only two minutes pass, but it feels like forever as my eyes slowly start to shut. Before I can convince my brain not to allow my head to lie on Landon's shoulder, my exhaustion takes over. I fall fast asleep on his shoulder, yet, I'm somehow still awake, because I can almost hear him looking at me strangely.

CHAPTER 20

Touched by an Angel

"**H**ey, Andy, get up." I hear, and feel, Leslie poking my head from behind. I rub my eyes to see Leon and Landon staring at me from each direction. For a minute there I almost forgot I was in Leon's car.

"What?" I groan, turning my head towards Leslie.

"We're home," Leslie informs me, unbuckling her seatbelt.

I look out the windshield and see Julian outside of the car, holding Tom, and opening our apartment building door. Landon scoots out the passenger seat so I can get out. I slide my butt out of the car, and by the time I'm all the way out, Leslie's already inside with Julian and Tom. Once again, they leave me behind.

"Thanks for the ride," I call out to Leon as I'm walking away.

Leon nods his head to tell me that I'm welcome. I turn and keep shuffling over to the building when I hear Landon call out.

"Yeah, and thanks for the drool," he chuckles, wiping his shoulder.

I ignore him, trying to keep my face from turning red, and grab the door handle. As I swing open the door someone taps my back. I swoosh around to see Nash standing next to me. I stare at him in silence, waiting for him to say something once again. It feels like I've been doing a lot of that lately.

"Thanks for — uh — everything." Nash kicks the little pebbles on the ground.

"What do you mean?" I question.

"Even though it was a bad weekend, it was one of the best," he grumbles.

"Oh. Um. You're welcome? See you tomorrow," I stutter, and begin to open the door. I pull open the door and rush into the building. Ah. Finally. Air conditioning.

I feel a gust of hot air from behind me and see Nash following me into the building. What does he want now?

"Andy, wait." Nash grabs me and spins me around.

I try to say something, but Nash hushes me before I can. He leans forward and kisses me on the lips. I've been waiting for this moment my whole life, and even though my lips are as dry and as cracked as can be, it feels as if I've just been touched by an angel.

I look at him in confusion and gleefulness. What just happened? Nash smiles at me, and for once, I'm not the one blushing.

"I just had to do that." He grins, and glides out of the building, hopping back into Leon's Mercedes Benz.

I stand there, stunned by what just happened, and watch the car drive out of the parking lot. Even though Nash's lies make me trust him a little less, I could honestly never deny the joy of that kiss. Plus, Nash had good intentions. He also just kissed me, meaning he clearly has a fantastic taste in women. So, that's a well-earned brownie point for him.

As I run up the stairs, I can still feel my lips tingling. I head over to apartment 21W with a smirk on my face. When I open the door, I see Julian and Leslie already asleep on the pull-out couch with a bag of tortilla chips tucked under Julian's arm.

Being back home in our little apartment makes me so happy. I look around at the silver walls and the blue flooring. I love this place, and I've missed it so much. From the strange wooden fridge, to the way it smells of rusted iron and memories. This will forever be my home; the place I'll always feel safe.

I pull the bag of chips out from underneath Julian's grip and eat the rest of the crumbs. Despite my lack of energy, I sing in the shower for about fifteen minutes.

When I step out of the shower, the entire bathroom is filled with humidity from the steam of the hot water. I sigh; I am so done with the heat right now. Trying to get away from the heat as quickly as possible, I throw on some loose shorts to act as pajamas.

"Finally." I breathe a sigh of relief as I sprawl myself out on Julian's recliner.

CHAPTER 21

The Puppet Master

"**O**h my gosh, Andy. I almost forgot about you."

I open my eyes and see Leslie standing in the doorway with her backpack slung over her shoulder. Though my vision is still blurry, I can tell Julian is standing next to her. I sit up, getting a small cramp in my lower back from the position I was in.

"Forgot about me? What?"

"We have to leave early for school. We're taking the bus there," I hear Julian's deep voice say.

I rub my eyes and yawn.

"And why are we taking the bus?" I ask as I walk into the bathroom to change my clothes. I hear Leslie say something, but I can't make it out. I throw on some jean shorts and an American flag tank top.

As I come out of the bathroom, both Julian and Leslie have their arms crossed.

"What'd you say? Sorry. I was getting dressed."

"We don't have the station wagon, and we're gonna be late. Let's go."

I roll my eyes at my own forgetfulness and grab my racecar backpack before I follow Julian and Leslie out the door, whining that my back hurts from sleeping in the recliner.

"Now you know how I feel," Julian chuckles.

"Just promise me I won't have to sleep in that ever again."

"No promises there, Andrea Lynn Brookes," Leslie says with a giggle.

She only ever calls me by my first name when she's trying to be funny. Usually I wouldn't laugh, because I hate my full name, but this time, I do laugh. It feels like we're getting back to our normal lives again.

On our way to the bus stop, I tell Julian and Leslie about Nash being a double agent. Both of them took it surprisingly well. Julian just thought it was lame and another reason, according to him, why rich people suck. As if only rich people could be double agents. Leslie then convinced him that it was super cool to be a double agent. Julian, who was taken aback by Leslie's charm, spent the first two minutes on the bus talking about how he wanted to befriend Nash now.

Five minutes into the bus ride, I find myself lost in thought, looking out the window. Julian and Leslie are sitting in front of me, and I have this nice, uncomfortable green seat all to myself.

As I look out the window, I see the little playground I saw the day I was suspended from school. It seems like so long ago. Seeing the playground again reminds me of how

I felt that day. I just wanted to find Leslie; I wanted her to be home. On that day, I had no idea what the future had in store. Now, looking at everything that has happened, I feel different. I feel stronger; physically and mentally. Physically because of how muscular my legs have gotten from all of that running. They honestly look like a dancer's legs. Mentally, though, I feel a lot more confident. Going through losing Leslie, and then finding her, being held captive in a small room, and even the kiss Nash gave me last night raised my confidence a little, too.

My happy thoughts are knocked from head when I see a guy with a cane on the side of the street. I know it's not Vincent, but seeing a cane shakes my emotions a bit.

A while later, I feel the bus come to a stop. *Great, time for school.* I see Julian and Leslie getting off of the bus, so I follow behind them. Looking at the school, I suddenly want to get to class. I know it's weird, but I kind of missed school. School gives me a sensation of normalcy, and that's all I want right now. Sometimes I just wish I didn't have supernatural abilities. Don't get me wrong, my powers are amazing, and, most of the time, they end up saving my life. But to be honest, sometimes I feel like the only reason I get into trouble in the first place is because of them.

Julian and Leslie split up, both going to their first hour classes. I grab my Algebra notebook and head over to my class. I smile as I walk in because I know that Nash will be in here.

When the bell rings, I sit down into a cold chair and open my notebook. I start to doodle pictures of little cartoon people surfing.

"Ahem," I hear a grueling voice cough.

I look up from my notebook. "Huh?"

Mrs. Santos is standing in front of my desk and glaring at me. I shut my notebook and look up at her.

"What's the problem, Mrs. Santos?"

"You've missed a lot of school lately," she growls, "And so has he." She points over to Nash.

I gulp, and the whole classroom laughs.

"Sorry. I was busy. And it was only like, a day."

"Yeah, same here," Nash says.

Mrs. Santos walks back towards the front of the room and sighs. I hear her say something rude about me under her breath, but I ignore it. She can say whatever she wants about me; it's not my fault I was being harassed by Vincent for the past few days.

"Get back to working with your partners. This is the last day to work on the assignment," Mrs. Santos drones a few minutes later.

Nash walks over to the seat in front of me and sits down.

"Well, shoot. We're so behind on this assignment."

"It's not really our fault," I reply, "We were busy being Vincent's puppets."

"Puppets?"

"Yeah. He treated us like puppets. He acted like we should do whatever he wants us to do."

"That's actually the perfect word to describe him. The Puppet Master," Nash agrees, "I'm sick of his puppet shows."

I nod my head with a smirk and we finally decide to get started on our assignment. It takes us the entire hour, but we finish the paper and turn it in. It may not be the best paper

I've ever written, but, considering the time in which we had to do it, it's acceptable.

By the time lunch arrives, I'm feeling exhausted. I forget how tiring school can be. Even though I'm exhausted, I'm still in a relatively good mood. Just the thought of being free from Vincent is a nice thought. I can't help but think he's coming back to get us, though.

I grab my lunch, which Leslie had packed for me while I was sleeping, and walk towards the cafeteria. I see Julian and Leslie sitting by the dumpsters, and I plop down next to them.

"Are you guys as tired as I am?"

"What'd you say? I couldn't hear you because I was starting to fall asleep," Julian jokes.

Leslie giggles, complimenting his humor.

"Really, Leslie?" I say, dumping out the contents of my lunch: a small bag of tortilla chips.

"We have to go grocery shopping soon," she says, laughing once again, and Julian joins her.

"How are you guys so calm right now? I can't stop thinking about Vincent."

"Come on, Andy. If he was going to come back for us, he would've done it by now." Julian puts a hand on my shoulder.

"I guess you're right."

Though I said he's right, I don't think he is. What is going to happen when Vincent does come back? We definitely need to think of a plan sooner rather than later.

When lunch is almost over with, someone catches my eye; it's Victoria. She's sitting next to Nash at a table far away from us. How could Nash stand to be with her right now? Especially after everything her father has done. I hope he's trying to get more information so we can take down Victoria's family once and for all.

As I watch her fling her long, blonde hair over her shoulder and laugh, I start to think about how I left her in that janitor's closet. *How in the world did she ever get out of there?* Nash had her tied to that chair pretty tight. Now that I think of it, why did Victoria forgive Nash for tying her up? If someone tied me to a chair, I wouldn't be laughing with them a few days later. Maybe he convinced her that it was necessary to make us, Nepos, trust him.

CHAPTER 22

Coconut Berry Juice

When I'm walking out of the cafeteria, Nash comes up behind me.

"Hey, cutie."

My mind jumbles. *Did he just call me cutie?* Holy schnitzel. No matter the number of obstacles Nash and I have, and will, conquer together, I'll still get butterflies anytime he compliments me.

"Uh, hey."

"Is that kiss still on your mind?" He grins. "It's still on mine."

His arrogant comment throws me off a little, but I ignore it. A smidge of arrogance never hurt anybody. Well, yeah, it probably has. But Nash wears it very well. He could wear anything and look like a million dollars.

Stopping myself from picturing Nash as an underwear model, I answer, "What? No."

He smiles at me. He can most likely tell by my face that I'm lying. I just hope he can't tell what I was thinking about.

"I saw you sitting with Victoria. What was that about?" I say, already acting like his jealous girlfriend. Luckily, he doesn't seem to notice my nosiness.

"I was apologizing to her for tying her up. I don't think she knows that her dad kidnapped Leslie."

"She does know. I heard her talking to him on the phone in the bathroom," I inform.

"Oh. I'm not sure, then. She seemed like she was acting pretty nice for once."

"She's probably trying to get closer to you so she can get closer to me."

"Maybe."

After our conversation about the horrendous Victoria, Nash and I separate and go to our fourth period classes.

In both fourth and fifth periods, I find myself almost falling asleep.

As I'm walking out of sixth period, Victoria shoots me an evil glare. I smile at her and make my way over to my locker. I put in the combination and the locker swings open. I put away my notebook, binder, and pencil, and grab my backpack.

I feel someone standing behind me.

"Hurry up, Leslie wants to get to the beach before everyone else."

I turn around to see Julian waiting impatiently.

"Before everyone else?" I ask.

"There's a party tonight."

"Okay, okay. I'm coming."

Julian and I make our way down the crowded hall.

"Since when does Leslie like parties?" I say, opening the door to the courtyard.

As we walk into the parking lot, Julian shrugs, "I think she just wants to get her mind off of you-know-who."

"Vincent?"

"Yup."

"I think we all need to get our minds off him."

Julian and I walk through the parking lot. I see our empty parking spot, where the station wagon is usually parked. A sad feeling crawls over me; I miss that car. I don't know if we'll ever get it back from that museum parking lot; it seems so far away.

I see Leslie leaning on a palm tree and fixing her dark hair into a pony tail.

"Andy, this party is going to be amaze-balls," Leslie says as she looks over at me.

We start to walk along the sidewalk, and the sun shines directly into my eyes; I've just about had it with this intense heat.

"There are going to be kegs and everything," Julian adds.

I pause, gathering my thoughts.

"Neither of you is worried about Vincent finding us there? Shouldn't we be in hiding, or something?"

"Of course we're worried about him. But, there's not much we can do about him," Leslie says.

"So we're just going to ignore the fact that he kidnapped you?"

"No, we're not. We'll come up with a plan tonight after the party," Julian backs Leslie up.

The three of us walk together, side by side. This time, instead of walking behind them, I walk beside them on the grass.

After a while, we finally arrive at the beach. I see people scattered everywhere. Most of them are in their bathing suits, but a few of them are in lifeguard uniforms. I'm glad we have lifeguards here. A lot of these people will be too drunk to stand by the end of the night, let alone swim.

"Tell me why this party is on a school night, again?" I glance at Julian and Leslie. "Seriously, you guys?"

The two of them are already over by the surf shack, ordering food. I angrily dig my feet into the hot, white sand. Ow.

After I make my way over, I plop myself onto a stool next to Leslie. She's drinking a smoothie, like usual.

"Coconut Berry Juice, please," I bark at a worker behind the counter.

"Uh, sorry. We're all out of that tonight."

"Oh, okay," I sigh. I hope that's not a bad omen.

"Would you like anything else?"

"No, thanks."

I notice Julian and Leslie laughing at me.

"What?"

"Poor Andrea doesn't get her favorite drink for once," Julian chuckles while holding Leslie's waist.

"Hey, be quiet. I came to this party for you guys. Don't make me leave."

Leslie scoots closer to me and whispers, "We can't split up, Andy. We're more vulnerable to him that way."

"To whom? Vincent: your father?"

"Don't say his name."

Leslie drinks the rest of her smoothie as if it's a shot. Though I wish to say more, I keep my mouth shut. Leslie seems to be in a good mood, and I don't want to ruin that for her.

It's ironic to me that Leslie said earlier we couldn't split up, because a few hours later, I find myself sitting alone at the surf shack. Julian and Leslie are in the water, enjoying themselves. I watch them as they splash each other and laugh as if there is not a care in the world.

When I look at Leslie on this beach, all I can think about is the night Vincent took her. *How is she not afraid of this place?* This beach definitely brings up some frightening memories for me. The way Leslie hung over Vincent's shoulder as he ran away from Julian and me. She looked so scared. I'll never forget the way she was that night. She was almost as innocent as we were when we were children, before we knew about our powers.

An hour later, I look back at the water, where Julian and Leslie are still splashing each other.

I stand up from the stool. "Well, see you later," I say as I read the cashier's nametag, "Patrick."

He awkwardly waves at me as I walk away. I'm pretty sure I scared him with my pointless babbling.

I head over to water, giving a nod to Julian as he sees me coming.

"Can we go home now? I'm super tired."

"I'm getting sort of tired, too," Leslie says before splashing Julian once more.

He splashes her back, and they start giggling again.

I sigh. "Come on, guys. I'm exhausted, and you said we shouldn't split up."

"Okay, fine. Let's go," Julian finally responds.

We all head back to our apartment in the dark. As we walk together, it almost feels like we're right back where we started. I'm just hoping that the whole sticky note situation doesn't happen again.

We make our way into the apartment building and bounce up the stairs to apartment 21W. Julian unlocks the door, and he and Leslie dive onto the pull-out couch.

"Hey, I thought the recliner was a one-time thing."

They both ignore my comment, so, hesitantly, I sit down onto the recliner. Despite the lumpiness of the chair, I soon fall asleep.

CHAPTER 23

Never Give Up

When I wake up, I see Julian holding Tom with drenched fur. Either Tom took a shower, or it rained. I'm guessing it rained. It's strange, though. The past few days it has rained a couple times, and it hardly ever rains.

"What time is it?" I hear Leslie ask Julian.

"9:35," I answer, sitting up. Wow. I've been sleeping for a really long time.

Leslie smiles at me, showing way too many teeth, and far too much gum.

"I think it's finally over," she voices, "I think Vincent's finally done messing with us."

"I doubt it," Julian utters from the kitchen.

I fully agree with Julian, but I don't want to put Leslie in a bad mood, so I smile and add, "Yeah, you're probably right, Leslie."

She bounces up and down excitedly and grabs a grocery bag full of cereal and hands it to me.

I slide out a giant box of Fruity Pebbles. Once I'm done with my dry cereal, I realize something: we have school today.

"Oh my gosh, you guys. School started at eight."

Julian gets a huge smile on his face. "It was cancelled. Flood and a heat wave."

Strange. A flood and a heat wave? I ponder silently in my head.

"Weren't we supposed to go to detention after school yesterday?" I ask. Since we missed more than one day of school, that means we are supposed to have detention for a week.

"Oh, crap. We were distracted by the party," Leslie says.

"You were distracted, not me. I knew about detention; I just didn't want to go," Julian chuckles.

Leslie hits Julian and scowls. She's such a goody-two-shoes sometimes.

I decide not to get dressed today. I mean, what's the point? No school. I'm excited about not having school and everything, but, even when I try, I can't stop thinking about Vincent coming back for us, and I know Julian's thinking the same thing.

After a few hours of chatting with Julian and Leslie, well, more like 'eating everything with Julian and Leslie,' we hear a pound on the door. Uh. Seriously? Who could be at the door at one in the afternoon?

Julian and Leslie look frightened, so I get up and slowly creep over to the door. I turn the doorknob, suddenly feeling frightened, too. When I squeak open the door, it's not who I expect it to be.

I look up at a tall, muscular body, with amazingly soft hair and blue eyes; it's Nash. My pulse slows down, and the thought of Vincent being at the door is erased from my mind as I gaze into Nash's eyes.

"What are you doing here?" I ask.

"I just came to ask if you want to go for a quick surf with me. The rain is supposed to let up for a little while. Julian and Leslie can come too, if they want."

"Sure, we'll come!" Leslie squeaks from behind me.

I hear Julian sigh, and I can only imagine the look on her face right now. She is probably grinning from ear to ear at the fact that Nash is here to see me.

"Let me grab my stuff." I smile. "You can wait inside."

"All right, cool." Nash enters and takes a seat on the couch, next to Julian.

I go into the bathroom and throw on a cute polka dot bikini, not that it will matter, though; it will be covered up by my wetsuit soon enough.

When all of us find our surfboards and swimsuits, we follow Nash into his shiny convertible. *Oh, boy, I've missed this car,* I think, as Nash holds the passenger door open for me.

I look back at Julian and smile; I remember his comment from earlier about rich people. Julian grins back at me; he knows what my smile is about.

"Did I miss something?" Leslie asks.

"Nope," I assure her.

She always gets mad when Julian and I have inside jokes without her, so I won't tell her about it just to bother her.

The convertible zooms out of the parking lot and the wind twists my hair into a tangled mess. Even though my hair is currently being destroyed of its just-brushed quality, I love the feeling of the wind. It makes me feel alive, almost as alive as I felt when we saved ourselves from falling into that gut-wrenching waterfall.

When we drive onto the beach, I see an infinity of red cups that are dug into the sand.

"Someone had a good time here," Nash jokes.

"I saw it first hand," I say, stepping out of the car.

"You guys were here last night? I heard it was a great party."

"Yeah, we were. It was fun," Leslie answers, bragging.

"You should've come," Julian says, patting Nash on the back.

I love seeing Julian being nice to Nash. It's almost like they're . . . friends? Julian has no guy friends. My best friend and my, hopefully, soon-to-be-boyfriend are unknowingly becoming buddies. This is great.

I stumble over a cup on the ground as I pull my surfboard from the back of the convertible. I'm surprised that Julian and Leslie fit back here with all of these surfboards.

"I'll beat you guys to the water," I challenge, running towards the shore.

Julian, Nash, and Leslie all grab their surfboards and chase after me. I jump into the dark blue water and start paddling. Sure enough, I'm the first one to get a big wave without cheating. I stand on my board and balance. As I'm surfing the wave, I almost get sucked under. I avoid the undertow and paddle over to shallow water.

I sit up on my board. "You guys were too scared to ride that wave?"

The three of them paddle over to me and laugh.

"We just wanted to see if you could do it," Leslie answers, "We all know I'm the best."

"Oh, please."

"I'll buy food for anyone who doesn't fall on this next wave," Nash offers.

"Am I included in that? I could really use a corn dog right about now," Julian questions.

Leslie splashes Julian. "We just ate a ton of food."

I giggle. Typical Julian, always wanting more to eat. We sit on our boards and talk for a little while. As we're talking, I look down at my board. Etched into the purple stripe, I can see a really, really small crack from whoever repaired my board.

"Look at this."

Julian paddles closer to me. "That could be from when I hit it with the station wagon."

"Yeah, true."

"Speaking of that, where is that crappy old car?" Nash asks.

None of us takes offense to Nash's comment. We all know it's crappy and old.

"Still sitting at the museum. We have no way to get it back."

We all laugh at how dumb we are.

When Julian and Leslie have had enough of surfing, they paddle back to the shore. Nash and I stay in the water, sitting on our boards. Nash slides off of his board and into the water. He drags his board along with him, as it is attached to his foot. He pulls himself up onto my board, behind me. My board wobbles and I look back at him.

"What are you doing?"

"Sitting on your board."

I laugh. "I know that. But, why?"

"I wanted to be alone with you."

"You're the one who invited Julian and Leslie to come with us."

"I didn't mean it," he says, moving my wet hair from lying on my back.

I turn my body around and face him. When I look at him, my heart races. It feels like I'm back in the day when I first saw him; the day everything changed for me. From that day forward, I had a hopeless crush on someone who would never even notice me. But now, now everything was different. He knows who I am, and I think he might even like me. Well, I'm pretty positive he does. You never know with boys, though.

"You look so beautiful right now, Andrea."

I try not to choke on my words. "I look like a mess. I'm covered in salt water and seaweed. Not to mention this hideous wetsuit."

"If you're a mess, you're my mess." He tucks my hair behind my ear and I smile.

"I'd be glad to be your mess."

Nash leans towards me and my eyes widen; he's going to kiss me again. I feel his lips on mine and I can taste the salt water. Usually I hate the taste, but right now, I love it.

Though the thought of Vincent is still in the back of my mind, I ignore it. I know I will have to deal with him at some point, but for now, I will just enjoy this. From this point forward, I will enjoy all of the little things in life. From Julian's witty remarks, to Leslie's rude, but loving, comments, and now, I'll even get to enjoy Nash and his perfect kisses.

As Nash and I paddle back to shore, all I can think about is the last thing my mom ever said to me: *Never give up. Even when your enemies give you no choice but to resign, don't do it. Family is all you need to make it through even the roughest of times.*

Printed in the United States
By Bookmasters